William Faulkner

REQUIEM FOR A NUN

William Cuthbert Faulkner was born in 1897 in New Albany, Mississippi, the first of four sons of Murry and Maud Butler Falkner (he later added the "u" to the family name himself). In 1904 the family moved to the university town of Oxford, Mississippi, where Faulkner was to spend most of his life. He was named for his great-grandfather "The Old Colonel," a Civil War veteran who built a railroad, wrote a bestselling romantic novel called *The White Rose of Memphis*, became a Mississippi state legislator, and was eventually killed in what may or may not have been a duel with a disgruntled business partner. Faulkner identified with this robust and energetic ancestor and often said that he inherited the "ink stain" from him.

Never fond of school, Faulkner left at the end of football season his senior year of high school, and began working at his grandfather's bank. In 1918, after his plans to marry his sweetheart Estelle Oldham were squashed by their families, he tried to enlist as a pilot in the U.S. Army but was rejected because he did not meet the height and weight requirements. He went to Canada, where he pretended to be an Englishman and joined the RAF training program there. Although he did not complete his training until after the war ended and never saw combat, he returned to his hometown in uniform, boasting of war wounds. He briefly attended the University of Mississippi, where he began to publish his poetry.

After spending a short time living in New York, he again returned to Oxford, where he worked at the university post office. His first book, a collection of poetry, *The Marble Faun*, was published at Faulkner's own expense in 1924. The writer Sherwood Anderson, whom he met in New Orleans in 1925, encouraged him to try writing fiction, and his first novel, *Soldier's Pay*, was published in 1926. It was followed by *Mosquitoes*. His next novel, which he titled *Flags in the Dust*, was rejected by his publisher and twelve others to whom he submitted it. It was eventually published in drastically edited form as *Sartoris* (the original version was not issued until after his death). Meanwhile, he was writing *The Sound and the Fury*, which, after being rejected by one publisher, came out in 1929 and received many ecstatic reviews, although it sold poorly. Yet again, a new novel, *Sanctuary*, was initially rejected by his publisher, this time as "too shocking." While working on the night shift at a power plant, Faulkner wrote what he was determined would be his masterpiece, *As I Lay Dying*. He finished it in about seven weeks, and it was published in 1930, again to generally good reviews and mediocre sales.

In 1929 Faulkner had finally married his childhood sweetheart, Estelle, after her divorce from her first husband. They had a premature daughter, Alabama, who died ten days after birth in 1931; a second daughter, Jill, was born in 1933.

With the eventual publication of his most sensational and violent (as well as, up till then, most successful) novel, *Sanctuary* (1931), Faulkner was invited to write scripts for MGM and Warner Brothers, where he was responsible for much of the dialogue in the film versions of Hemingway's *To Have and Have Not* and Chandler's *The Big Sleep*, and many other films. He continued to write novels and published many stories in the popular magazines. *Light in August* (1932) was his first attempt to address the racial issues of the South, an effort continued in *Absalom, Absalom!* (1936), and *Go Down, Moses* (1942). By 1946, most of Faulkner's novels were out of print in the United States (although they remained well-regarded in Europe), and he was seen as a minor, regional writer. But then the influential editor and critic Malcolm Cowley, who had earlier championed Hemingway and Fitzgerald and others of their generation, put together the *Portable Faulkner*, and once again Faulkner's genius was recognized, this time for good. He received the 1949 Nobel Prize for Literature as well as many other awards and accolades, including the National Book Award and the Gold Medal from the American Academy of Arts and Letters and France's Legion of Honor.

In addition to several collections of short fiction, his other novels include *Pylon* (1935), *The Unvanquished* (1938), *The Wild Palms* (1939), *The Hamlet* (1940), *Intruder in the Dust* (1948), *A Fable* (1954), *The Town* (1957), *The Mansion* (1959), and *The Reivers* (1962).

William Faulkner died of a heart attack on July 6, 1962, in Oxford, Mississippi, where he is buried.

REQUIEM FOR A NUN

BOOKS BY WILLIAM FAULKNER

The Marble Faun (1924)

Soldier's Pay (1926)

Mosquitoes (1927)

Sartoris (1929) [*Flags in the Dust* (1973)]

The Sound and the Fury (1929)

As I Lay Dying (1930)

Sanctuary (1931)

These 13 (1931)

Light in August (1932)

A Green Bough (1933)

Doctor Martino and Other Stories (1934)

Pylon (1935)

Absalom, Absalom! (1936)

The Unvanquished (1938)

The Wild Palms [*If I Forget Thee, Jerusalem*] (1939)

The Hamlet (1940)

Go Down, Moses and Other Stories (1942)

Intruder in the Dust (1948)

Knight's Gambit (1949)

Collected Stories of William Faulkner (1950)

Notes on a Horsethief (1951)

Requiem for a Nun (1954)

A Fable (1954)

Big Woods (1955)

The Town (1957)

The Mansion (1959)

The Reivers (1962)

Uncollected Stories of William Faulkner (1979, Posthumous)

William Faulkner

REQUIEM FOR A NUN

VINTAGE INTERNATIONAL

Vintage Books

A Division of Random House, Inc.

New York

FIRST VINTAGE INTERNATIONAL EDITION, NOVEMBER 2011

Library of Congress Cataloging-in-Publication Data
Faulkner, William, 1897–1962.
Requiem for a nun.
I. Title.
PZ.F272Rj5 PS3511.A86
813'.5'2
74-17145

Vintage ISBN: 978-0-307-94680-5

www.vintagebooks.com

CONTENTS

PUBLISHER'S NOTE

This edition of *Requiem for a Nun* follows the text as corrected in 1994 by Noel Polk. The copy-text for this edition is the ribbon typescript setting copy at the Alderman Library of the University of Virginia. An editors' note on the corrections by Noel Polk follows the text; the line and page notes were prepared by Joseph Blotner.

REQUIEM FOR A NUN

ACT I

The Courthouse

(A NAME FOR THE CITY)

T he courthouse is less old than the town, which began somewhere under the turn of the century as a Chickasaw Agency trading-post and so continued for almost thirty years before it discovered, not that it lacked a depository for its records and certainly not that it needed one, but that only by creating or anyway decreeing one, could it cope with a situation which otherwise was going to cost somebody money;

The settlement had the records; even the simple dispossession of Indians begot in time a minuscule of archive, let alone the normal litter of man's ramshackle confederation against environment—that time and that wilderness;—in this case, a meagre, fading, dogeared, uncorrelated, at times illiterate sheaf of land grants and patents and transfers and deeds, and tax- and militia-rolls, and bills of sale for slaves, and counting-house lists of spurious currency and exchange rates, and liens and mortgages, and listed rewards for escaped or stolen Negroes and other livestock, and diary-like annotations of births and marriages and deaths and public hangings and land-auctions, accumulating slowly for those three decades in a sort of iron pirate's chest in the back room of the postoffice-tradingpost-store, until that day thirty years later when, because of a jailbreak compounded by an ancient monster iron padlock transported a

thousand miles by horseback from Carolina, the box was removed to a small new leanto room like a wood- or tool-shed
built two days ago against one outside wall of the morticed-log
mud-chinked shake-down jail; and thus was born the Yoknapatawpha County courthouse: by simple fortuity, not only less
old than even the jail, but come into existence at all by chance
and accident: the box containing the documents not moved
from any place, but simply to one; removed from the trading-
post back room not for any reason inherent in either the back
room or the box, but on the contrary: which — the box — was not
only in nobody's way in the back room, it was even missed when
gone since it had served as another seat or stool among the
powder- and whiskey-kegs and firkins of salt and lard about the
stove on winter nights; and was moved at all for the simple reason that suddenly the settlement (overnight it would become a
town without having been a village; one day in about a hundred
years it would wake frantically from its communal slumber into
a rash of Rotary and Lion Clubs and Chambers of Commerce
and City Beautifuls: a furious beating of hollow drums toward
nowhere, but merely to sound louder than the next little human
clotting to its north or south or east or west, dubbing itself city as
Napoleon dubbed himself emperor and defending the expedi-
ent by padding its census rolls — a fever, a delirium in which it
would confound forever seething with motion and motion with
progress. But that was a hundred years away yet; now it was frontier, the men and women pioneers, tough, simple, and durable,
seeking money or adventure or freedom or simple escape, and
not too particular how they did it.) discovered itself faced not so
much with a problem which had to be solved, as a Damocles
sword of dilemma from which it had to save itself;

Even the jailbreak was fortuity: a gang—three or four—of
Natchez Trace bandits (twenty-five years later legend would

begin to affirm, and a hundred years later would still be at it, that two of the bandits were the Harpes themselves, Big Harpe anyway, since the circumstances, the method of the breakout left behind like a smell, an odor, a kind of gargantuan and bizarre playfulness at once humorous and terrifying, as if the settlement had fallen, blundered, into the notice or range of an idle and whimsical giant. Which—that they were the Harpes— was impossible, since the Harpes and even the last of Mason's ruffians were dead or scattered by this time, and the robbers would have had to belong to John Murrel's organization—if they needed to belong to any at all other than the simple fraternity of rapine.) captured by chance by an incidental band of civilian more-or-less militia and brought in to the Jefferson jail because it was the nearest one, the militia band being part of a general muster at Jefferson two days before for a Fourth of July barbecue, which by the second day had been refined by hardy elimination into one drunken brawling which rendered even the hardiest survivors vulnerable enough to be ejected from the settlement by the civilian residents, the band which was to make the capture having been carried, still comatose, in one of the evicting wagons to a swamp four miles from Jefferson known as Hurricane Bottoms, where they made camp to regain their strength or at least their legs, and where that night the four—or three—bandits, on their way across country to their hideout from their last exploit on the Trace, stumbled onto the campfire. And here report divided; some said that the sergeant in command of the militia recognised one of the bandits as a deserter from his corps, others said that one of the bandits recognised in the sergeant a former follower of his, the bandit's, trade. Anyway, on the fourth morning all of them, captors and prisoners, returned to Jefferson in a group, some said in confederation now seeking more drink, others said that the captors brought their prizes back to the settlement

in revenge for having been evicted from it. Because these were
frontier, pioneer, times, when personal liberty and freedom
were almost a physical condition like fire or flood, and no community was going to interfere with anyone's morals as long as
the amoralist practised somewhere else, and so Jefferson, being
neither on the Trace nor the River but lying about midway between, naturally wanted no part of the underworld of either;

But they had some of it now, taken as it were by surprise, un-
awares, without warning to prepare and fend off. They put the
bandits into the log-and-mudchinking jail, which until now
had had no lock at all since its clients so far had been ama-
teurs—local brawlers and drunkards and runaway slaves—for
whom a single heavy wooden beam in slots across the outside
of the door like on a corncrib, had sufficed. But they had now
what might be four—three—Dillingers or Jesse Jameses of the
time, with rewards on their heads. So they locked the jail; they
bored an auger hole through the door and another through the
jamb and passed a length of heavy chain through the holes and
sent a messenger on the run across to the postoffice-store to
fetch the ancient Carolina lock from the last Nashville mail-
pouch—the iron monster weighing almost fifteen pounds,
with a key almost as long as a bayonet, not just the only lock in
that part of the country, but the oldest lock in that cranny of
the United States, brought there by one of the three men who
were what was to be Yoknapatawpha County's coeval pioneers
and settlers, leaving in it the three oldest names—Alexander
Holston, who came as half groom and half bodyguard to Doctor Samuel Habersham, and half nurse and half tutor to the
doctor's eight-year-old motherless son, the three of them riding
horseback across Tennessee from the Cumberland Gap along
with Louis Grenier, the Huguenot younger son who brought
the first slaves into the country and was granted the first big

land patent and so became the first cotton planter; while Doctor Habersham, with his worn black bag of pills and knives and his brawny taciturn bodyguard and his half orphan child, became the settlement itself (for a time, before it was named, the settlement was known as Doctor Habersham's, then Habersham's, then simply Habersham; a hundred years later, during a schism between two ladies' clubs over the naming of the streets in order to get free mail delivery, a movement was started, first, to change the name back to Habersham; then, failing that, to divide the town in two and call one half of it Habersham after the old pioneer doctor and founder)—friend of old Issetibbeha, the Chickasaw chief (the motherless Habersham boy, now a man of twenty-five, married one of Issetibbeha's grand-daughters and in the thirties emigrated to Oklahoma with his wife's dispossessed people), first unofficial, then official Chickasaw agent until he resigned in a letter of furious denunciation addressed to the President of the United States himself; and—his charge and pupil a man now— Alexander Holston became the settlement's first publican, establishing the tavern still known as the Holston House, the original log walls and puncheon floors and hand-morticed joints of which are still buried somewhere beneath the modern pressed glass and brick veneer and neon tubes. The lock was his:

Fifteen pounds of useless iron lugged a thousand miles through a desert of precipice and swamp, of flood and drouth and wild beasts and wild Indians and wilder white men, displacing that fifteen pounds better given to food or seed to plant food or even powder to defend with, to become a fixture, a kind of landmark, in the bar of a wilderness ordinary, locking and securing nothing, because there was nothing behind the heavy bars and shutters needing further locking and securing;

not even a paper weight because the only papers in the Holston House were the twisted spills in an old powder horn above
the mantel for lighting tobacco; always a little in the way, since
it had constantly to be moved: from bar to shelf to mantel then
back to bar again until they finally thought about putting it on
the bi-monthly mail-pouch; familiar, known, presently the oldest unchanged thing in the settlement, older than the people
since Issetibbeha and Doctor Habersham were dead, and
Alexander Holston was an old man crippled with arthritis, and
Louis Grenier had a settlement of his own on his vast plantation, half of which was not even in Yoknapatawpha County,
and the settlement rarely saw him; older than the town, since
there were new names in it now even when the old blood ran
in them—Sartoris and Stevens, Compson and McCaslin and
Sutpen and Coldfield—and you no longer shot a bear or deer
or wild turkey simply by standing for a while in your kitchen
door, not to mention the pouch of mail—letters and even
newspapers—which came from Nashville every two weeks by
a special rider who did nothing else and was paid a salary for it
by the Federal government; and that was the second phase of
the monster Carolina lock's transubstantiation into the Yoknapatawpha County courthouse;

The pouch didn't always reach the settlement every two weeks,
nor even always every month. But sooner or later it did, and
everybody knew it would, because it—the cowhide saddlebag
not even large enough to hold a full change of clothing, containing three or four letters and half that many badly-printed
one- and two-sheet newspapers already three or four months
out of date and usually half and sometimes wholly misin-
formed or incorrect to begin with—was the United States, the
power and the will to liberty, owning liegence to no man,
bringing even into that still almost pathless wilderness the thin

peremptory voice of the nation which had wrenched its freedom from one of the most powerful peoples on earth and then
again within the same lifespan successfully defended it; so
peremptory and audible that the man who carried the pouch
on the galloping horse didn't even carry any arms except a tin
horn, traversing month after month, blatantly, flagrantly, almost contemptuously, a region where for no more than the
boots on his feet, men would murder a traveller and gut him
like a bear or deer or fish and fill the cavity with rocks and sink
the evidence in the nearest water; not even deigning to pass
quietly where other men, even though armed and in parties,
tried to move secretly or at least without uproar, but instead an-
nouncing his solitary advent as far ahead of himself as the ring
of the horn would carry. So it was not long before Alexander
Holston's lock had moved to the mail-pouch. Not that the
pouch needed one, having come already the three hundred
miles from Nashville without a lock. (It had been projected at
first that the lock remain on the pouch constantly. That is, not
just while the pouch was in the settlement, but while it was on
the horse between Nashville and the settlement too. The rider
refused, succinctly, in three words, one of which was printable.
His reason was the lock's weight. They pointed out to him that
this would not hold water, since not only—the rider was a frail
irascible little man weighing less than a hundred pounds—
would the fifteen pounds of lock even then fail to bring his
weight up to that of a normal adult male, the added weight of
the lock would merely match that of the pistols which his employer, the United States government, believed he carried and
even paid him for having done so, the rider's reply to this being
succinct too though not so glib: that the lock weighed fifteen
pounds either at the back door of the store in the settlement, or
at that of the postoffice in Nashville. But since Nashville and
the settlement were three hundred miles apart, by the time the

horse had carried it from one to the other, the lock weighed
fifteen pounds to the mile times three hundred miles, or forty-
five hundred pounds. Which was manifest nonsense, a physical impossibility either in lock or horse. Yet indubitably fifteen
pounds times three hundred miles was forty-five hundred
something, either pounds or miles,—especially as while they
were still trying to unravel it, the rider repeated his first three
succinct—two unprintable—words.) So less than ever would
the pouch need a lock in the back room of the trading-post,
surrounded and enclosed once more by civilization, where its
very intactness, its presence to receive a lock, proved its lack of
that need during the three hundred miles of rapine-haunted
Trace; needing a lock as little as it was equipped to receive one,
since it had been necessary to slit the leather with a knife just
under each jaw of the opening and insert the lock's iron
mandible through the two slits and clash it home, so that any
other hand with a similar knife could have cut the whole lock
from the pouch as easily as it had been clasped onto it. So the
old lock was not even a symbol of security: it was a gesture of
salutation, of free men to free men, of civilization to civilization across not just the three hundred miles of wilderness to
Nashville, but the fifteen hundred to Washington: of respect
without servility, allegiance without abasement to the government which they had helped to found and had accepted with
pride but still as free men, still free to withdraw from it at any
moment when the two of them found themselves no longer
compatible, the old lock meeting the pouch each time on its
arrival, to clasp it in iron and inviolable symbolism, while old
Alec Holston, childless bachelor, grew a little older and grayer,
a little more arthritic in flesh and temper too, a little stiffer and
more rigid in bone and pride too, since the lock was still his, he
had merely lent it, and so in a sense he was the grandfather in
the settlement of the inviolability not just of government mail,

but of a free government of free men too, so long as the government remembered to let men live free, not under it but beside it;

That was the lock; they put it on the jail. They did it quickly, not even waiting until a messenger could have got back from the Holston House with old Alec's permission to remove it from the mail-pouch or use it for the new purpose. Not that he would have objected on principle nor refused his permission except by simple instinct; that is, he would probably have been the first to suggest the lock if he had known in time or thought of it first, but he would have refused at once if he thought the thing was contemplated without consulting him. Which everybody in the settlement knew, though this was not at all why they didn't wait for the messenger. In fact, no messenger had ever been sent to old Alec; they didn't have time to send one, let alone wait until he got back; they didn't want the lock to keep the bandits in, since (as was later proved) the old lock would have been no more obstacle for the bandits to pass than the customary wooden bar; they didn't need the lock to protect the settlement from the bandits, but to protect the bandits from the settlement. Because the prisoners had barely reached the settlement when it developed that there was a faction bent on lynching them at once, out of hand, without preliminary— a small but determined gang which tried to wrest the prisoners from their captors while the militia was still trying to find someone to surrender them to, and would have succeeded except for a man named Compson, who came to the settlement a few years ago with a race-horse, which he swapped to Ikkemotubbe, Issetibbeha's successor in the chiefship, for a square mile of what was to be the most valuable land in the future town of Jefferson, who, legend said, drew a pistol and held the ravishers at bay until the bandits could be got into the jail and

the auger holes bored and someone sent to fetch old Alec Holston's lock. Because there were indeed new names and faces
too in the settlement now—faces so new as to have (to the
older residents) no discernible antecedents other than mam-
malinity, nor past other than the simple years which had
scored them; and names so new as to have no discernible (nor
discoverable either) antecedents or past at all, as though they
had been invented yesterday, report dividing again: to the effect that there were more people in the settlement that day
than the militia sergeant whom one or all of the bandits might
recognise;

So Compson locked the jail, and a courier with the two best
horses in the settlement—one to ride and one to lead—cut
through the woods to the Trace to ride the hundred-odd miles
to Natchez with news of the capture and authority to dicker for
the reward; and that evening in the Holston House kitchen was
held the settlement's first municipal meeting, prototype not
only of the town council after the settlement would be a town,
but of the chamber of commerce when it would begin to pro-
claim itself a city, with Compson presiding, not old Alec, who
was quite old now, grim, taciturn, sitting even on a hot July
night before a smoldering log in his vast chimney, his back
even turned to the table (he was not interested in the deliberation; the prisoners were his already since his lock held them;
whatever the conference decided would have to be submitted
to him for ratification anyway before anyone could touch his
lock to open it) around which the progenitors of the Jefferson
city fathers sat in what was almost a council of war, not only discussing the collecting of the reward, but the keeping and defending it. Because there were two factions of opposition now:
not only the lynching party, but the militia band too, who now
claimed that as prizes the prisoners still belonged to their orig-

inal captors; that they—the militia—had merely surrendered
the prisoners' custody but had relinquished nothing of any reward: on the prospect of which, the militia band had got more
whiskey from the trading-post store and had built a tremendous
bonfire in front of the jail, around which they and the lynching
party had now confederated in a wassail or conference of their
own. Or so they thought. Because the truth was, that Compson, in the name of a crisis in the public peace and welfare,
had made a formal demand on the professional bag of Doctor
Peabody, old Doctor Habersham's successor, and the three of
them—Compson, Peabody, and the post trader (his name was
Ratcliffe; a hundred years later it would still exist in the county,
but by that time it had passed through two inheritors who had
dispensed with the eye in the transmission of words, using only
the ear, so that by the time the fourth one had been compelled
by simple necessity to learn to write it again, it had lost the 'c'
and the final 'fe' too) added the laudanum to the keg of
whiskey and sent it as a gift from the settlement to the aston-
ished militia sergeant, and returned to the Holston House
kitchen to wait until the last of the uproar died; then the law-
and-order party made a rapid sortie and gathered up all the comatose opposition, lynchers and captors too, and dumped
them all into the jail with the prisoners and locked the door
again and went home to bed—until the next morning, when
the first arrivals were met by a scene resembling an outdoor
stage setting: which was how the legend of the mad Harpes
started: a thing not just fantastical but incomprehensible, not
just whimsical but a little terrifying (though at least it was
bloodless, which would have contented neither Harpe): not
just the lock gone from the door nor even just the door gone
from the jail, but the entire wall gone, the mud-chinked axe-
morticed logs unjointed neatly and quietly in the darkness and
stacked as neatly to one side, leaving the jail open to the world

like a stage on which the late insurgents still lay sprawled and various in deathlike slumber, the whole settlement gathered now to watch Compson trying to kick at least one of them awake, until one of the Holston slaves—the cook's husband, the waiter-groom-hostler—ran into the crowd shouting, 'Whar de lock, whar de lock, ole Boss say whar de lock.'

It was gone (as were three horses belonging to three of the lynching faction). They couldn't even find the heavy door and the chain, and at first they were almost betrayed into believing that the bandits had had to take the door in order to steal the chain and lock, catching themselves back from the very brink of this wanton accusation of rationality. But the lock was gone; nor did it take the settlement long to realise that it was not the escaped bandits and the aborted reward, but the lock, and not a simple situation which faced them, but a problem which threatened, the slave departing back to the Holston House at a dead run and then reappearing at the dead run almost before the door, the walls, had had time to hide him, engulf and then eject him again, darting through the crowd and up to Compson himself now, saying, 'Ole Boss say fetch de lock'——not send the lock, but bring the lock. So Compson and his lieutenants (and this was where the mail rider began to appear, or rather, to emerge—the fragile wisp of a man ageless hairless and toothless, who looked too frail even to approach a horse, let alone ride one six hundred miles every two weeks, yet who did so, and not only that but had wind enough left not only to announce and precede but even follow his passing with the jeering musical triumph of the horn:—a contempt for possible—probable—despoilers matched only by that for the official dross of which he might be despoiled, and which agreed to remain in civilised bounds only so long as the despoilers had the taste to refrain)—repaired to the kitchen where old Alec still sat before his smoldering log, his back still to the room, and still not turning it this time either. And that was all. He ordered the immediate return of his lock. It was not even an ultimatum, it was a simple instruction, a decree, impersonal, the mail rider now well into the fringe of the group, saying nothing and missing nothing, like a weightless desiccated or fossil bird, not a vulture of course nor even quite a hawk, but say a pterodactyl chick arrested just out of the egg ten glaciers ago and so old in simple infancy as to be worn and weary ancestor of all subsequent life. They pointed out to old Alec that the only reason the lock could be missing was that the bandits had not had time or been able to cut it out of the door, and that even three fleeing madmen on stolen horses would not carry a six-foot oak door very far, and that a party of Ikkemotubbe's young men were even now trailing the horses westward toward the River and that without doubt the lock would be found at any moment, probably under the first bush at the edge of the settlement: knowing better, knowing that there was no limit to the fantastic and the terrifying and the bizarre, of which the men were capable who already, just to escape from a log jail, had quietly removed one entire wall and stacked it in neat piecemeal at the roadside, and that they nor old Alec neither would ever see his lock again;

Nor did they; the rest of that afternoon and all the next day too, while old Alec still smoked his pipe in front of his smoldering log, the settlement's sheepish and raging elders hunted for it, with (by now: the next afternoon) Ikkemotubbe's Chickasaws helping too, or anyway present, watching: the wild men, the wilderness's tameless evictant children looking only the more wild and homeless for the white man's denim and butternut and felt and straw which they wore, standing or squatting or following, grave attentive and interested, while the white men sweated and cursed among the bordering thickets of their punily-clawed foothold; and always the rider, Pettigrew, ubiquitous, everywhere, not helping search himself and never in anyone's way, but always present, inscrutable, saturnine, missing nothing: until at last toward sundown Compson crashed savagely out of the last bramble-brake and flung the sweat from his face with a full-armed sweep sufficient to repudiate a throne, and said,

'All right, god damn it, we'll pay him for it.' Because they had already considered that last gambit; they had already realised its seriousness from the very fact that Peabody had tried to make a joke about it which everyone knew that even Peabody did not think humorous:

'Yes——and quick too, before he has time to advise with Pettigrew and price it by the pound.'

'By the pound?' Compson said.

'Pettigrew just weighed it by the three hundred miles from Nashville. Old Alec might start from Carolina. That's fifteen thousand pounds.'

'Oh,' Compson said. So he blew in his men by means of a foxhorn which one of the Indians wore on a thong around his neck, though even then they paused for one last quick conference; again it was Peabody who stopped them.

'Who'll pay for it?' he said. 'It would be just like him to want a dollar a pound for it, even if by Pettigrew's scale he had found it in the ashes of his fireplace.' They—Compson anyway—had probably already thought of that; that, as much as Pettigrew's presence, was probably why he was trying to rush them into old Alec's presence with the offer so quickly that none would have the face to renege on a pro rata share. But Peabody had torn it now. Compson looked about at them, sweating, grimly enraged.

'That means Peabody will probably pay one dollar,' he

said. 'Who pays the other fourteen? Me?' Then Ratcliffe, the
trader, the store's proprietor, solved it—a solution so simple, so
limitless in retroact, that they didn't even wonder why nobody
had thought of it before; which not only solved the problem
but abolished it; and not just that one, but all problems, from
now on into perpetuity, opening to their vision like the rending
of a veil, like a glorious prophecy, the vast splendid limitless
panorama of America: that land of boundless opportunity, that
bourne, created not by nor of the people, but for the people, as
was the heavenly manna of old, with no return demand on
man save the chewing and swallowing since out of its own
matchless Allgood it would create produce train support and
perpetuate a race of laborers dedicated to the single purpose of
picking the manna up and putting it into his lax hand or even
between his jaws,—illimitable, vast, without beginning or end,
not even a trade or a craft but a beneficence as are sunlight and
rain and air, inalienable and immutable.

'Put it on the Book,' Ratcliffe said—the Book: not a ledger,
but *the* ledger, since it was probably the only thing of its kind
between Nashville and Natchez, unless there might happen to
be a similar one a few miles south at the first Chocktaw agency
at Yalo Busha,—a ruled, paper-backed copybook such as might
have come out of a schoolroom, in which accrued, with the
United States as debtor, in Mohataha's name (the Chickasaw
matriarch, Ikkemotubbe's mother and old Issetibbeha's sister,
who—she could write her name, or anyway make something
with a pen or pencil which was agreed to be, or at least accepted to be, a valid signature—signed all the conveyances as
her son's kingdom passed to the white people, regularising it in
law anyway) the crawling tedious list of calico and gunpowder,
whiskey and salt and snuff and denim pants and osseous candy
drawn from Ratcliffe's shelves by her descendants and subjects
and Negro slaves. That was all the settlement had to do: add

the lock to the list, the account. It wouldn't even matter at what price they entered it. They could have priced it on Pettigrew's scale of fifteen pounds times the distance not just to Carolina but to Washington itself, and nobody would ever notice it probably; they could have charged the United States with seventeen thousand five hundred dollars worth of the fossilised and indestructible candy, and none would ever read the entry. So it was solved, done, finished, ended. They didn't even have to discuss it. They didn't even think about it anymore, unless perhaps here and there to marvel (a little speculatively probably) at their own moderation, since they wanted nothing—least of all, to escape any just blame—but a fair and decent adjustment of the lock. They went back to where old Alec still sat with his pipe in front of his dim hearth. Only they had overestimated him; he didn't want any money at all, he wanted his lock. Whereupon what little remained of Compson's patience went too.

'Your lock's gone,' he told old Alec harshly. 'You'll take fifteen dollars for it,' he said, his voice already fading, because even that rage could recognise impasse when it saw it. Nevertheless, the rage, the impotence, the sweating, the *too much*—whatever it was—forced the voice on for one word more: 'Or——' before it stopped for good and allowed Peabody to fill the gap:

'Or else?' Peabody said, and not to old Alec, but to Compson. 'Or else what?' Then Ratcliffe saved that too.

'Wait,' he said. 'Uncle Alec's going to take fifty dollars for his lock. A guarantee of fifty dollars. He'll give us the name of the blacksmith back in Cal'lina that made it for him, and we'll send back there and have a new one made. Going and coming and all'll cost about fifty dollars. We'll give Uncle Alec the fifty dollars to hold as a guarantee. Then when the new lock comes, he'll give us back the money. All right, Uncle Alec?' And that could have been all of it. It probably would have been, except for Pettigrew. It was not that they had forgotten him, nor even assimilated him. They had simply sealed—healed him off (so they thought)—him into their civic crisis as the desperate and defenseless oyster immobilises its atom of inevictable grit. Nobody had seen him move yet he now stood in the center of them where Compson and Ratcliffe and Peabody faced old Alec in the chair. You might have said that he had oozed there, except for that adamantine quality which might (in emergency) become invisible but never insubstantial and never in this world fluid; he spoke in a voice bland, reasonable and impersonal, then stood there being looked at, frail and childsized, impermeable as diamond and manifest with portent, bringing into that backwoods room a thousand miles deep in pathless wilderness, the whole vast incalculable weight of federality, not just representing the government nor even himself just the government; for that moment at least, he was the United States.

'Uncle Alec hasn't lost any lock,' he said. 'That was Uncle Sam.'

After a moment someone said, 'What?'

'That's right,' Pettigrew said. 'Whoever put that lock of Holston's on that mail bag either made a voluntary gift to the United States, and the same law covers the United States government that covers minor children: you can give something to them, but you cant take it back, or he or they done something else.'

They looked at him. Again after a while somebody said something; it was Ratcliffe. 'What else?' Ratcliffe said. Pettigrew answered, still bland, impersonal, heatless and glib:

'Committed a violation of act of Congress as especially made and provided for the defacement of government property, penalty of five thousand dollars or not less than one year

in a Federal jail or both. For whoever cut them two slits in the
bag to put the lock in, act of Congress as especially made and
provided for the injury or destruction of government property,
penalty of ten thousand dollars or not less than five years in a
Federal jail or both.' He did not move even yet; he simply
spoke directly to old Alec: 'I reckon you're going to have supper
here same as usual sooner or later or more or less.'

'Wait,' Ratcliffe said. He turned to Compson. 'Is that true?'

'What the hell difference does it make whether it's true or
not?' Compson said. 'What do you think he's going to do as
soon as he gets to Nashville?' He said violently to Pettigrew:
'You were supposed to leave for Nashville yesterday. What
were you hanging around here for?'

'Nothing to go to Nashville for,' Pettigrew said. 'You dont
want any mail. You aint got anything to lock it up with.'

'So we aint,' Ratcliffe said. 'So we'll let the United States
find the United States' lock.' This time Pettigrew looked at no
one. He wasn't even speaking to anyone, anymore than old
Alec had been when he decreed the return of his lock:

'Act of Congress as made and provided for the unautho-
rised removal and or use or willful or felonious use or misuse
or loss of government property, penalty the value of the article
plus five hundred to ten thousand dollars or thirty days to
twenty years in a Federal jail or both. They may even make a
new one when they read where you have charged a postoffice
department lock to the bureau of Indian affairs.' He moved;
now he was speaking to old Alec again: 'I'm going out to my
horse. When this meeting is over and you get back to cooking,
you can send your nigger for me.'

Then he was gone. After a while Ratcliffe said, 'What do
you reckon he aims to get out of this? A reward?' But that was
wrong; they all knew better than that.

'He's already getting what he wants,' Compson said, and

cursed again. 'Confusion. Just damned confusion.' But that was wrong too; they all knew that too, though it was Peabody who said it:

'No. Not confusion. A man who will ride six hundred miles through this country every two weeks, with nothing for protection but a foxhorn, aint really interested in confusion any more than he is in money.' So they didn't know yet what was in Pettigrew's mind. But they knew what he would do. That is, they knew that they did not know at all, either what he would do, or how, or when, and that there was nothing whatever that they could do about it until they discovered why. And they saw now that they had no possible means to discover that; they realised now that they had known him for three years now, during which, fragile and inviolable and undeviable and preceded for a mile or more by the strong sweet ringing of the horn, on his strong and tireless horse he would complete the bi-monthly trip from Nashville to the settlement and for the next three or four days would live among them, yet that they knew nothing whatever about him, and even now knew only that they dared not, simply dared not, take any chance, sitting for a while longer in the darkening room while old Alec still smoked, his back still squarely turned to them and their quandary too; then dispersing to their own cabins for the evening meal—with what appetite they could bring to it, since presently they had drifted back through the summer darkness when by ordinary they would have been already in bed, to the back room of Ratcliffe's store now, to sit again while Ratcliffe recapitulated in his mixture of bewilderment and alarm (and something else which they recognised was respect as they realised that he—Ratcliffe—was unshakably convinced that Pettigrew's aim was money; that Pettigrew had invented or evolved a scheme so richly rewarding that he—Ratcliffe—had not only been unable to forestall him and do it first, he—Ratcliffe—

couldn't even guess what it was after he had been given a hint) until Compson interrupted him.

'Hell,' Compson said. 'Everybody knows what's wrong with him. It's ethics. He's a damned moralist.'

'Ethics?' Peabody said. He sounded almost startled. He said quickly: 'That's bad. How can we corrupt an ethical man?'

'Who wants to corrupt him?' Compson said. 'All we want him to do is stay on that damned horse and blow whatever extra wind he's got into that damned horn.'

But Peabody was not even listening. He said, 'Ethics,' almost dreamily. He said, 'Wait.' They watched him. He said suddenly to Ratcliffe: 'I've heard it somewhere. If anybody here knows it, it'll be you. What's his name?'

'His name?' Ratcliffe said. 'Pettigrew's? Oh. His christian name.' Ratcliffe told him. 'Why?'

'Nothing,' Peabody said. 'I'm going home. Anybody else coming?' He spoke directly to nobody and said and would say no more, but that was enough: a straw perhaps, but at least a straw; enough anyway for the others to watch and say nothing either as Compson got up to and said to Ratcliffe,

'You coming?' and the three of them walked away together, beyond earshot then beyond sight too. Then Compson said, 'All right. What?'

'It may not work,' Peabody said. 'But you two will have to back me up. When I speak for the whole settlement, you and Ratcliffe will have to make it stick. Will you?'

Compson cursed. 'But at least tell us a little of what we're going to guarantee.' So Peabody told them, some of it, and the next morning entered the stall in the Holston House stable where Pettigrew was grooming his ugly hammerheaded iron-muscled horse.

'We decided not to charge that lock to old Mohataha, after all,' Peabody said.

'That so?' Pettigrew said. 'Nobody in Washington would ever catch it. Certainly not the ones that can read.'

'We're going to pay for it ourselves,' Peabody said. 'In fact, we're going to do a little more. We've got to repair that jail wall anyhow; we've got to build one wall anyway. So by building three more, we will have another room. We got to build one anyway, so that dont count. So by building an extra three-wall room, we will have another four-wall house. That will be the courthouse.' Pettigrew had been hissing gently between his teeth at each stroke of the brush, like a professional Irish groom. Now he stopped, the brush and his hand arrested in midstroke, and turned his head a little.

'Courthouse?'

'We're going to have a town,' Peabody said. 'We already got a church—that's Whitfield's cabin. And we're going to build a school too soon as we get around to it. But we're going to build the courthouse today; we've already got something to put in it to make it a courthouse: that iron box that's been in Ratcliffe's way in the store for the last ten years. Then we'll have a town. We've already even named her.'

Now Pettigrew stood up, very slowly. They looked at one another. After a moment Pettigrew said, 'So?'

'Ratcliffe says your name's Jefferson,' Peabody said.

'That's right,' Pettigrew said. 'Thomas Jefferson Pettigrew. I'm from old Ferginny.'

'Any kin?' Peabody said.

'No,' Pettigrew said. 'My ma named me for him, so I would have some of his luck.'

'Luck?' Peabody said.

Pettigrew didn't smile. 'That's right. She didn't mean luck. She never had any schooling. She didn't know the word she wanted to say.'

'Have you had it?' Peabody said. Nor did Pettigrew smile

now. 'I'm sorry,' Peabody said. 'Try to forget it.' He said: 'We decided to name her Jefferson.' Now Pettigrew didn't seem to
breathe even. He just stood there, small, frail, less than boy-
size, childless and bachelor, incorrigibly kinless and tieless,
looking at Peabody. Then he breathed, and raising the brush,
he turned back to the horse and for an instant Peabody thought
he was going back to the grooming. But instead of making the
stroke, he laid the hand and the brush against the horse's flank
and stood for a moment, his face turned away and his head
bent a little. Then he raised his head and turned his face back
toward Peabody.

'You could call that lock "axle grease" on that Indian account,' he said.

'Fifty dollars worth of axle grease?' Peabody said.

'To grease the wagons for Oklahoma,' Pettigrew said.

'So we could,' Peabody said. 'Only her name's Jefferson
now. We cant ever forget that anymore now.' And that was the
courthouse—the courthouse which it had taken them almost
thirty years not only to realise they didn't have, but to discover
that they hadn't even needed, missed, lacked; and which, before they had owned it six months, they discovered was
nowhere near enough. Because somewhere between the dark
of that first day and the dawn of the next, something happened
to them. They began that same day; they restored the jail wall
and cut new logs and split out shakes and raised the little floorless lean-to against it and moved the iron chest from Ratcliffe's
back room; it took only the two days and cost nothing but the
labor and not much of that per capita since the whole settlement was involved to a man, not to mention the settlement's
two slaves—Holston's man and the one belonging to the German blacksmith—; Ratcliffe too, all he had to do was put up
the bar across the inside of his back door, since his entire pa-
tronage was countable in one glance sweating and cursing

among the logs and shakes of the half dismantled jail across the way opposite—including Ikkemotubbe's Chickasaws, though these were neither sweating nor cursing: the grave dark men dressed in their Sunday clothes except for the trousers, pants, which they carried rolled neatly under their arms or perhaps tied by the two legs around their necks like capes or rather hussars' dolmans where they had forded the creek, squatting or lounging along the shade, courteous, interested, and reposed (even old Mohataha herself, the matriarch, barefoot in a purple silk gown and a plumed hat, sitting in a gilt brocade empire chair in a wagon behind two mules, under a silver-handled Paris parasol held by a female slave child)—because they (the other white men, his confreres, or—during this first day—his co-victims) had not yet remarked the thing—quality—something—esoteric, eccentric, in Ratcliffe's manner, attitude,—not an obstruction nor even an impediment, not even when on the second day they discovered what it was, because he was among them, busy too, sweating and cursing too, but rather like a single chip, infinitesimal, on an otherwise unbroken flood or tide, a single body or substance alien and unreconciled, a single thin almost unheard voice crying thinly out of the roar of a mob: 'Wait, look here, listen——'

Because they were too busy raging and sweating among the dismantled logs and felling the new ones in the adjacent woods and trimming and notching and dragging them out and mixing the tenuous clay mud to chink them together with; it was not until the second day that they learned what was troubling Ratcliffe, because now they had time, the work going no slower, no lessening of sweat but on the contrary, if anything the work going even a little faster because now there was a lightness in the speed and all that was abated was the rage and the outrage, because somewhere between the dark and the dawn of the first and the second day, something had happened to them—the men who had spent that first long hot endless July day sweating and raging about the wrecked jail, flinging indiscriminately and savagely aside the dismantled logs and the log-like laudanum-smitten inmates in order to rebuild the one, cursing old Holston and the lock and the four—three—bandits and the eleven militiamen who had arrested them, and Compson and Pettigrew and Peabody and the United States of America,—the same men met at the project before sunrise on the next day which was already promising to be hot and endless too, but with the rage and the fury absent now, quiet, not grave so much as sobered, a little amazed, diffident, blinking a little perhaps, looking a little aside from one another, a little unfamiliar even to one another in the new jonquil-colored light, looking about them at the meagre huddle of crude cabins set without order and every one a little awry to every other and all dwarfed to dollhouses by the vast loom of the woods which enclosed them— the tiny clearing clawed punily not even into the flank of pathless wilderness but into the loin, the groin, the secret parts, which was the irrevocable cast die of their lives, fates, pasts and futures—not even speaking for a while yet since each one probably believed (a little shamefaced too) that the thought was solitarily his, until at last one spoke for all and then it was all right since it had taken one conjoined breath to shape that sound, the speaker speaking not loud, diffidently, tentatively, as you insert the first light tentative push of wind into the mouthpiece of a strange untried foxhorn: 'By God. Jefferson.'

'Jefferson, Mississippi,' a second added.

'Jefferson, Yoknapatawpha County, Mississippi,' a third corrected; who, which one, didn't matter this time either since it was still one conjoined breathing, one compound dream-state, mused and static, well capable of lasting on past sunrise too, though they probably knew better too since Compson was still there: the gnat, the thorn, the catalyst:

'It aint until we finish the goddamned thing,' Compson said. 'Come on. Let's get at it.' So they finished it that day, working rapidly now, with speed and lightness too, concentrated yet inattentive, to get it done and that quickly, not to finish it but to get it out of the way, behind them; not to finish it quickly in order to own, possess it sooner, but to be able to obliterate, efface, it the sooner, as if they had also known in that first yellow light that it would not be near enough, would not even be the beginning; that the little lean-to room they were building would not even be a pattern and could not even be called practice, working on until noon, the hour to stop and eat, by which time Louis Grenier had arrived from Frenchman's Bend (his plantation: his manor, his kitchens and stables and kennels and slave quarters and gardens and promenades and fields which a hundred years later will have vanished, his name and his blood too, leaving nothing but the name of his plantation and his own fading corrupted legend like a thin layer of the native ephemeral yet inevictable dust on a section of country surrounding a little lost paintless crossroads store) twenty miles away behind a slave coachman and footman in his imported English carriage and what was said to be the finest matched team outside of Natchez or Nashville, and Compson said, 'I reckon that'll do,'—all knowing what he meant: not abandonment: to complete it, of course, but so little remained now that the two slaves could finish it. The four in fact, since, although as soon as it was assumed that the two Grenier Negroes would lend the two local ones a hand, Compson demurred on the grounds that who would dare violate the rigid protocol of bondage by ordering a stable-servant, let alone a house-servant, to do manual labor, not to mention having the temerity to approach old Louis Grenier with the suggestion. Peabody nipped that at once.

'One of them can use my shadow,' he said. 'It never blenched out there with a white doctor standing in it,' and

even offered to be emissary to old Grenier, except that Grenier
himself forestalled them. So they ate Holston's noon ordinary,
while the Chickasaws, squatting unmoving still where the
creep of shade had left them in the full fierce glare of July
noon about the wagon where old Mohataha still sat under her
slave-borne Paris parasol, ate their lunches too which (Mohataha's and her personal retinue's came out of a woven white-
oak withe fishbasket in the wagonbed) they appeared to have
carried in from what, patterning the white people, they called
their plantation too, under their arms inside the rolled-up
trousers. Then they moved back to the front gallery and—not
the settlement anymore now: the town; it had been a town for
thirty-one hours now—watched the four slaves put up the final
log and pin down the final shake on the roof and hang the door
and then, Ratcliffe leading something like the court chamber-
lain across a castle courtyard, cross back to the store and enter
and emerge carrying the iron chest, the grave Chickasaws
watching too the white man's slaves sweating the white man's
ponderable dense inscrutable medicine into its new shrine.
And now they had time to find out what was bothering Ratcliffe.

'That lock,' Ratcliffe said.

'What?' somebody said.

'That Indian axle grease,' Ratcliffe said.

'What?' they said again. But they knew, understood, now.
It was neither lock nor axle grease; it was the fifteen dollars
which could have been charged to the Indian Department on
Ratcliffe's books and nobody would have ever found it, noticed
it, missed it. It was not greed on Ratcliffe's part, and least of all
was he advocating corruption. The idea was not even new to
him; it did not need any casual man on a horse riding in to the
settlement once every two or three weeks, to reveal to him that
possibility; he had thought of that the first time he had charged
the first sack of peppermint candy to the first one of old Mo-

hataha's forty-year-old grandchildren and had refrained from
adding two zeroes to the ten or fifteen cents for ten years now,
wondering each time why he did refrain, amazed at his own
virtue or at least his strength of will. It was a matter of principle.
It was he—they: the settlement (town now)—who had thought
of charging the lock to the United States as a provable lock, a
communal risk, a concrete ineradicable object, win lose or
draw, let the chips fall where they may on that dim day when
some federal inspector might, just barely might, audit the
Chickasaw affairs; it was the United States itself which had
voluntarily offered to show them how to transmute the inevictable lock into proofless and ephemeral axle grease—the
little scrawny childsized man, solitary unarmed impregnable
and unalarmed, not even defying them, not even advocate and
representative of the United States, but *the* United States, as
though the United States had said, 'Please accept a gift of fifteen dollars,' (the town had actually paid old Alec fifteen dollars for the lock; he would accept no more) and they had not
even declined it but simply abolished it since, as soon as Pettigrew breathed it into sound, the United States had already forever lost it; as though Pettigrew had put the actual ponderable
fifteen gold coins into—say, Compson's or Peabody's—hands
and they had dropped them down a rathole or a well, doing no
man any good, neither restoration to the ravaged nor emolu-
ment to the ravager, leaving in fact the whole race of man, as
long as it endured, forever and irrevocably fifteen dollars
deficit, fifteen dollars in the red;

That was Ratcliffe's trouble. But they didn't even listen. They
heard him out of course, but they didn't even listen. Or perhaps they didn't even hear him either, sitting along the shade
on Holston's gallery, looking, seeing, already a year away; it was
barely the tenth of July; there was the long summer, the bright
soft dry fall until the November rains, but they would require

not two days this time but two years and maybe more, with a winter of planning and preparation before hand. They even had an instrument available and waiting, like providence almost: a man named Sutpen who had come into the settlement that same spring—a big gaunt friendless passion-worn untalkative man who walked in a fading aura of anonymity and violence like a man just entered a warm room or at least a shelter, out of a blizzard, bringing with him thirty-odd men slaves even wilder and more equivocal than the native wild men, the Chickasaws, to whom the settlement had become accustomed, who (the new Negroes) spoke no English but instead what Compson, who had visited New Orleans, said was the Carib-Spanish-French of the Sugar Islands, and who (Sutpen) had bought or proved on or anyway acquired a tract of land in the opposite direction and was apparently bent on establishing a place on an ever more ambitious and grandiose scale than Grenier's; he had even brought with him a tame Parisian architect—or captive rather, since it was said in Ratcliffe's back room that the man slept at night in a kind of pit at the site of the chateau he was planning, tied wrist to wrist with one of his captor's Carib slaves; indeed, the settlement had only to see him once to know that he was no dociler than his captor, any more than the weasel or rattlesnake is no less untame than the wolf or bear before which it gives way until completely and hopelessly cornered:—a man no larger than Pettigrew, with humorous sardonic undefeated eyes which had seen everything and believed none of it, in the broad expensive hat and brocaded waistcoat and ruffled wrists of a half-artist half-boulevardier; and they—Compson perhaps, Peabody certainly—could imagine him in his mudstained brier-slashed brocade and lace standing in a trackless wilderness dreaming colonnades and porticoes and fountains and promenades in the style of David, with just behind each elbow an identical

giant half-naked Negro not even watching him, only breathing, moving each time he took a step or shifted like his shadow
repeated in two and blown to gigantic size;

So they even had an architect. He listened to them for perhaps
a minute in Ratcliffe's back room. Then he made an inde-
scribable gesture and said, 'Bah. You do not need advice. You
are too poor. You have only your hands, and clay to make good
brick. You dont have any money. You dont even have anything
to copy: how can you go wrong?' But he taught them how to
mold the brick; he designed and built the kiln to bake the brick
in, plenty of them since they had probably known from that
first yellow morning too that one edifice was not going to be
enough. But although both were conceived in the same instant
and planned simultaneously during the same winter and built
in continuation during the next three years, the courthouse of
course came first, and in March, with stakes and hanks of fishline, the architect laid out in a grove of oaks opposite the tavern and the store, the square and simple foundations, the
irrevocable design not only of the courthouse but of the town
too, telling them as much: 'In fifty years you will be trying to
change it in the name of what you will call progress. But you
will fail; but you will never be able to get away from it.' But
they had already seen that, standing thigh-deep in wilderness
also but with more than a vision to look at since they had at
least the fishline and the stakes, perhaps less than fifty years,
perhaps—who knew?—less than twenty-five even: a Square,
the courthouse in its grove the center; quadrangular around it,
the stores, two storey, the offices of the lawyers and doctors and
dentists, the lodge-rooms and auditoriums, above them; school
and church and tavern and bank and jail each in its ordered
place; the four broad diverging avenues straight as plumb-lines
in the four directions, becoming the network of roads and by-

roads until the whole county would be covered with it: the
hands, the prehensile fingers clawing dragging lightward out of
the disappearing wilderness year by year as up from the bottom
of the receding sea, the broad rich fecund burgeoning fields,
pushing thrusting each year further and further back the
wilderness and its denizens—the wild bear and deer and
turkey, and the wild men (or not so wild anymore, familiar
now, harmless now, just obsolete: anachronism out of an old
dead time and a dead age; regrettable of course, even actually
regretted by the old men, fiercely as old Doctor Habersham
did, and with less fire but still as irreconciliable and stubborn
as old Alec Holston and a few others were still doing, until in a
few more years the last of them would have passed and vanished in their turn too, obsolescent too: because this was a
white man's land; that was its fate, or not even fate but destiny,
its high destiny in the roster of the earth);—the veins, arteries,
life- and pulse-stream along which would flow the aggrandise-
ment of harvest: the gold: the cotton and the grain;

But above all, the courthouse: the center, the focus, the hub;
sitting looming in the center of the county's circumference like
a single cloud in its ring of horizon, laying its vast shadow to the
uttermost rim of horizon; musing, brooding, symbolic and ponderable, tall as cloud, solid as rock, dominating all: protector of
the weak, judiciate and curb of the passions and lusts, reposi-
tory and guardian of the aspirations and the hopes; rising
course by brick course during that first summer, simply square,
simplest Georgian colonial (this, by the Paris architect who was
creating at Sutpen's Hundred something like a wing of Ver-
sailles glimpsed in a Lilliput's gothic nightmare—in revenge,
Gavin Stevens would say a hundred years later, when Sutpen's
own legend in the county would include the anecdote of the
time the architect broke somehow out of his dungeon and tried
to flee and Sutpen and his Negro headman and hunter ran him

down with dogs in the swamp and brought him back) since, as the architect had told them, they had no money to buy bad taste with nor even anything from which to copy what bad taste might still have been within their compass; this one too still costing nothing but the labor and—the second year now— most of that was slave since there were still more slave owners in the settlement which had been a town and named for going on two years now, already a town and already named when the first ones waked up on that yellow morning two years back:— men other than Holston and the blacksmith (Compson was one now) who owned one or two or three Negroes, besides Gre- nier and Sutpen who had set up camps beside the creek in Compson's pasture for the two gangs of their Negroes to live in until the two buildings—the courthouse and the jail—should be completed. But not altogether slave, the boundmen, the un- free, because there were still the white men too, the same ones who on that hot July morning two and now three years ago had gathered in a kind of outraged unbelief to fling, hurl up in rag- ing sweating impotent fury the little three-walled lean-to,—the same men (with affairs of their own they might have been at- tending to or work of their own or for which they were being hired, paid, that they should have been doing) standing or lounging about the scaffolding and the stacks of brick and pud- dles of clay mortar for an hour or two hours or half a day, then putting aside one of the Negroes and taking his place with trowel or saw or adze, unbidden or unreproved either since there was none present with the right to order or deny; a stranger might have said probably for that reason, simply be- cause now they didn't have to, except that it was more than that, working peacefully now that there was no outrage and fury, and twice as fast because there was no urgency since this was no more to be hurried by man or men than the burgeoning of a crop, working (this paradox too to anyone except men like Gre- nier and Compson and Peabody who had grown from infancy

among slaves, breathed the same air and even suckled the same
breast with the sons of Ham: black and white, free and unfree,
shoulder to shoulder in the same tireless lift and rhythm as if
they had the same aim and hope, which they did have as far as
the Negro was capable, as even Ratcliffe, son of a long pure line
of Anglo-Saxon mountain people and—destined—father of an
equally long and pure line of white trash tenant farmers who
never owned a slave and never would since each had and
would imbibe with his mother's milk a personal violent antipa-
thy not at all to slavery but to black skins, could have explained:
the slave's simple child's mind had fired at once with the
thought that he was helping to build not only the biggest edifice in the country, but probably the biggest he had ever seen;
this was all but this was enough) as one because it was theirs,
bigger than any because it was the sum of all and, being the
sum of all, it must raise all of their hopes and aspirations level
with its own aspirant and soaring cupola, so that, sweating and
tireless and unflagging, they would look about at one another a
little shyly, a little amazed, with something like humility too, as
if they were realising, or were for a moment at least capable of
believing, that men, all men, including themselves, were a little better, purer maybe even, than they had thought, expected,
or even needed to be. Though they were still having a little
trouble with Ratcliffe: the money, the Holston lock–Chickasaw
axle grease fifteen dollars; not trouble really because it had
never been an obstruction even three years ago when it was
new, and now after three years even the light impedeless chip
was worn by familiarity and custom to less than a toothpick:
merely present, merely visible, or that is, audible: and no trouble *with* Ratcliffe because he made one too contraposed the
toothpick; more: he was its chief victim, sufferer, since where
with the others was mostly inattention, a little humor, now and
then a little fading annoyance and impatience, with him was
shame, bafflement, a little of anguish and despair like a man

struggling with a congenital vice, hopeless, indomitable, already defeated. It was not even the money anymore now, the fifteen dollars. It was the fact that they had refused it and, refusing it, had maybe committed a fatal and irremediable error. He would try to explain it: 'It's like Old Moster and the rest of them up there that run the luck, would look down at us and say, Well well, looks like them durn peckerwoods down there dont want them fifteen dollars we was going to give them free-gratis-for-nothing. So maybe they dont want nothing from us. So maybe we better do like they seem to want, and let them sweat and swivet and scrabble through the best they can by themselves.'

Which they—the town—did, though even then the courthouse was not finished for another six years. Not but that they thought it was: complete: simple and square, floored and roofed and windowed, with a central hallway and the four offices—sheriff and tax assessor and circuit- and chancery-clerk (which—the chancery-clerk's office—would contain the ballot boxes and booths for voting)—below, and the courtroom and jury-room and the judge's chambers above,—even to the pigeons and English sparrows, migrants too but not pioneers, inevictably urban in fact, come all the way from the Atlantic coast as soon as the town became a town with a name, taking possession of the gutters and eave-boxes almost before the final hammer was withdrawn, uxorious and interminable the one, garrulous and myriad the other. Then in the sixth year old Alec Holston died and bequeathed back to the town the fifteen dollars it had paid him for the lock; two years before, Louis Grenier had died and his heirs still held in trust on demand the fifteen hundred dollars his will had devised it, and now there was another newcomer in the county, a man named John Sartoris, with slaves and gear and money too like Grenier and Sutpen, but who was an even better stalemate to Sutpen than Grenier had been because it was apparent at once that he, Sartoris, was the sort of

man who could even cope with Sutpen in the sense that a man
with a sabre or even a small sword and heart enough for it, could
cope with one with an axe; and that summer (Sutpen's Paris architect had long since gone back to whatever place he came
from and to which he had made his one abortive midnight try to
return, but his trickle, flow of bricks had never even faltered: his
molds and kilns had finished the jail and were now raising the
walls of two churches and by the half-century would have completed what would be known through all north Mississippi and
east Tennessee as *the* Academy, *the* Female Institute) there was
a committee: Compson and Sartoris and Peabody (and *in ab-
sentia* Sutpen: nor would the town ever know exactly how much
of the additional cost Sutpen and Sartoris made up): and the
next year the eight disjointed marble columns were landed
from an Italian ship at New Orleans, into a steamboat up the
Mississippi to Vicksburg, and into a smaller steamboat up the
Yazoo and Sunflower and Tallahatchie, to Ikkemotubbe's old
landing which Sutpen now owned, and thence the twelve miles
by oxen into Jefferson: the two identical four-column porticoes,
one on the north and one on the south, each with its balcony of
wrought-iron New Orleans grillwork, on one of which—the
south one—in 1861 Sartoris would stand in the first Confederate uniform the town had ever seen, while in the Square below
the Richmond mustering officer enrolled and swore in the regiment which Sartoris as its colonel would take to Virginia as a
part of Bee, to be Jackson's extreme left in front of the Henry
house at First Manassas, and from both of which each May and
November for a hundred years, bailiffs in their orderly ap-
pointive almost hereditary succession would cry without inflec-
tion or punctuation either 'oyes oyes honorable circuit court of
yoknapatawpha county come all and ye shall be heard' and beneath which for that same length of time too except for the
seven years between '63 and '70 which didn't really count a century afterward except to a few irreconciliable old ladies, the

white male citizens of the county would pass to vote for county and state offices, because when in '63 a United States military force burned the Square and the business district, the courthouse survived. It didn't escape: it simply survived: harder than axes, tougher than fire, more fixed than dynamite; encircled by the tumbled and blackened ruins of lesser walls, it still stood, even the topless smoke-stained columns, gutted of course and roofless, but immune, not one hair even out of the Paris architect's almost forgotten plumb, so that all they had to do (it took nine years to build; they needed twenty-five to restore it) was put in new floors for the two storeys and a new roof, and this time with a cupola with a four-faced clock and a bell to strike the hours and ring alarms; by this time the Square, the banks and the stores and the lawyers' and doctors' and dentists' offices, had been restored, and the English sparrows were back too which had never really deserted—the garrulous noisy independent swarms which, as though concomitant with, inextricable from regularised and roted human quarreling, had appeared in possession of cornices and gutter-boxes almost before the last nail was driven—and now the pigeons also, interminably murmurous, nesting in, already usurping, the belfry even though they couldn't seem to get used to the bell, bursting out of the cupola at each stroke of the hour in frantic clouds, to sink and burst and whirl again at each succeeding stroke, until the last one: then vanishing back through the slatted louvers until nothing remained but the frantic and murmurous cooing like the fading echoes of the bell itself, the source of the alarm never recognised and even the alarm itself unremembered, as the actual stroke of the bell is no longer remembered by the vibration-fading air. Because they—the sparrows and the pigeons—endured, durable, a hundred years, the oldest things there except the courthouse centennial and serene above the town most of whose people now no longer even knew who Doctor Habersham and old Alec Holston and Louis Grenier were, had been; centennial and serene above the change: the electricity and gasoline, the neon and the crowded cacophonous air; even Negroes passing in beneath the balconies and into the chancery clerk's office to cast ballots too, voting for the same white-skinned rascals and demagogues and white supremacy champions that the white ones did,—durable: every few years the county fathers, dreaming of bakhshish, would instigate a movement to tear it down and erect a new modern one, but someone would at the last moment defeat them; they will try it again of course and be defeated perhaps once again or even maybe twice again, but no more than that. Because its fate is to stand in the hinterland of America: its doom is its longevity; like a man, its simple age is its own reproach, and after the hundred years, will become unbearable. But not for a little while yet; for a little while yet the sparrows and the pigeons: garrulous myriad and independent the one, the other uxorious and interminable, at once frantic and tranquil—until the clock strikes again which even after a hundred years, they still seem unable to get used to, bursting in one swirling explosion out of the belfry as though the hour, instead of merely adding one puny infinitesimal more to the long weary increment since Genesis, had shattered the virgin pristine air with the first loud dingdong of time and doom.

SCENE I

Courtroom. 5:30 P.M. November thirteenth.

The Curtain is down. As the lights begin to go up:

MAN'S VOICE (*behind the curtain*)
    Let the prisoner stand.

The curtain rises, symbolising the rising of the prisoner in the dock, and revealing a section of the courtroom. It does not occupy the whole stage, but only the upper left half, leaving the other half and the bottom of the stage in darkness, so that the visible scene is not only spotlighted but elevated slightly too, a further symbolism which will be clearer when Act II opens— the symbolism of the elevated tribunal of justice of which this, a County court, is only the intermediate, not the highest, stage.

This is a section of the court—the bar, the judge, officers, the opposing lawyers, the jury. The defense lawyer is Gavin Stevens, about fifty. He looks more like a poet than a lawyer and actually is: a bachelor, descendant of one of the pioneer Yoknapatawpha County families, Harvard and Heidelberg educated, and returned to his native soil to be a sort of bucolic Cincinnatus, champion not so much of truth as of justice, or of justice as he sees it, constantly involving himself, often for no pay, in affairs of equity and passion and even crime too among his people, white and Negro both, sometimes directly contrary to his office of County Attorney which he has held for years, as is the present business.

The prisoner is standing. She is the only one standing in the room—a Negress, quite black, about thirty—that is, she could be almost anything between twenty and forty—with a calm impenetrable almost bemused face, the tallest, highest there with all eyes on her but she herself not looking at any of them, but looking out and up as though at some distant corner of the room, as though she were alone in it. She is—or until recently, two months ago to be exact—a domestic servant, nurse to two white children, the second of whom, an infant, she smothered in its cradle two months ago, for which act she is now on trial for her life. But she has probably done many things else—

chopped cotton, cooked for working gangs—any sort of manual labor within her capacities, or rather, limitations in time and availability, since her principal reputation in the little Mississippi town where she was born is that of a tramp—a drunkard, a casual prostitute, being beaten by some man or cutting or being cut by his wife or his other sweetheart. She has probably been married, at least once. Her name—or so she calls it and would probably spell it if she could spell—is Nancy Mannigoe.

There is a dead silence in the room while everybody watches her.

JUDGE

Have you anything to say before the sentence of the court is pronounced upon you?

Nancy neither answers nor moves; she doesn't even seem to be listening.

JUDGE

That you, Nancy Mannigoe, did on the thirteenth day of September, wilfully and with malice aforethought kill and murder the infant child of Mr and Mrs Gowan Stevens in the town of Jefferson and the County of Yoknapatawpha . . . . . .

It is the sentence of this court that you be taken from hence back to the county jail of Yoknapatawpha County and there on the thirteenth day of March be hanged by the neck until you are dead. And may God have mercy on your soul.

NANCY (*quite loud in the silence, to no one, quite calm, not moving*)

Yes, Lord.

There is a gasp, a sound, from the invisible spectators in the room, of shock at this unheard-of violation of procedure: the beginning of something which might be consternation and even uproar, in the midst of, or rather above which, Nancy herself does not move. The judge bangs his gavel, the bailiff springs up, the curtain starts hurriedly and jerkily down as if the judge, the officers, the court itself were jerking frantically at it to hide this disgraceful business; from somewhere among the unseen spectators there comes the sound of a woman's voice—a moan, wail, sob perhaps.

BAILIFF (*loudly*)
    Order! Order in the court! Order!

The curtain descends rapidly, hiding the scene, the lights fade rapidly into darkness: a moment of darkness: then the curtain rises smoothly and normally on:

SCENE II

Stevens living-room. 6:00 P.M. November thirteenth.

Living-room, a center table with a lamp, chairs, a sofa left rear, floor-lamp, wall-bracket lamps, a door L enters from hall, double doors rear stand open on a dining-room, a fireplace R with gas logs. The atmosphere of the room is smart, modern, up-to-date, yet the room itself has the air of another time—the high ceiling, the cornices, some of the furniture; it has the air of being in an old house, an ante-bellum house descended at last to a spinster survivor who has modernised it (vide the gas fire and the two overstuffed chairs) into apartments rented to young couples or families who can afford to pay that much rent in order to live on the right street among other young couples who belong to the right church and the country club.

Sound of feet, then the lights come on as if someone about to enter had pressed a wall switch, then the door L opens and Temple enters, followed by Gowan, her husband, and the lawyer, Gavin Stevens. She is in the middle twenties, very smart, soignée, in an open fur coat, wearing a hat and gloves and carrying a handbag. Her air is brittle and tense, yet controlled. Her face shows nothing as she crosses to the center table and stops.

Gowan is three or four years older. He is almost a type; there were many of him in America, the South, between the two great wars: only children of financially secure parents living in city apartment hotels, alumni of the best colleges, South or East, where they belonged to the right clubs; married now and raising families yet still alumni of their schools, performing acceptably jobs they themselves did not ask for, usually concerned with money: cotton futures, or stocks, or bonds. But this face is a little different, a little more than that. Something has happened to it—tragedy—something, against which it had had no warning, and to cope with which (as it discovered) no equipment, yet which it has accepted and is trying, really and sincerely and self-lessly (perhaps for the first time in its life) to do its best with according to its code. He and Stevens wear their overcoats, carrying their hats. Stevens stops just inside the room. Gowan drops his hat onto the sofa in passing and goes on to where Temple stands at the table, stripping off one of her gloves.

TEMPLE (*takes cigarette from box on the table: mimics the
         prisoner; her voice, harsh, reveals for the first time
         repressed, controlled, hysteria*)

Yes, God. Guilty, God. Thank you, God. If that's your
attitude toward being hung, what else can you expect
from a judge and jury except to accommodate you?

GOWAN

Stop it, Boots. Hush now. Soon as I light the fire, I'll
buy a drink.
        (to Stevens)
Or maybe Gavin will do the fire while I do the butler.

TEMPLE *(takes up lighter)*

I'll do the fire. You get the drinks. Then Uncle Gavin
wont have to stay. After all, all he wants to do is say,
Goodbye and send me a postcard. He can almost do
that in two words, if he tries hard. Then he can go
home.

She crosses to the hearth and kneels and turns the gas valve,
the lighter ready in her other hand.

GOWAN *(anxiously)*

Now, Boots.

TEMPLE *(snaps lighter, holds flame to the jet)*

Will you for God's sake please get me a drink?

GOWAN

Sure, honey.
        (he turns: to Stevens)
Drop your coat anywhere.

He exits into the dining-room. Stevens does not move, watching Temple as the log takes fire.

TEMPLE (*still kneeling, her back to Stevens*)
> If you're going to stay, why dont you sit down? Or vice versa. Backward. Only, it's the first one that's backward: if you're not sitting down, why dont you go? Let me be bereaved and vindicated, but at least let me do it in privacy, since God knows if any one of the excretions should take place in privacy, triumph should be the one ——

Stevens watches her. Then he crosses to her, taking the handkerchief from his breast pocket, stops behind her and extends the handkerchief down where she can see it. She looks at it, then up at him. Her face is quite calm.

TEMPLE
> What's that for?

STEVENS
> It's all right. It's dry too.
> (*still extending the handkerchief*)
> For tomorrow, then.

TEMPLE (*rises quickly*)
> Oh, for cinders. On the train. We're going by air; hadn't Gowan told you? We leave from the Memphis airport at midnight; we're driving up after supper. Then California tomorrow morning; maybe we'll even go on to Hawaii in the spring. No; wrong season: Canada, maybe. Lake Louise in May and June ——
> (*she stops, listens a moment toward the dining-room doors*)
> So why the handkerchief? Not a threat, because you dont have anything to threaten me with, do you? And

if you dont have anything to threaten me with, I must not have anything you want, so it cant be a bribe either, can it?

(they both hear the sound from beyond the dining-room doors which indicates that Gowan is approaching. Temple lowers her voice again, rapidly)

Put it this way then. I dont know what you want, because I dont care. Because whatever it is, you wont get it from me.

(the sound is near now—footsteps, clink of glass)

Now he'll offer you a drink, and then he'll ask you too what you want, why you followed us home. I've already answered you. No. If what you came for is to see me weep, I doubt if you'll even get that. But you certainly wont get anything else. Not from me. Do you understand that?

STEVENS

I hear you.

TEMPLE

Meaning, you dont believe it. All right, *touché* then.

(quicker, tenser)

I refused to answer your question; now I'll ask you one: How much do you—

(as Gowan enters, she changes what she was saying so smoothly in mid-sentence that anyone entering would not even realise that the pitch of her voice had altered)

—are her lawyer, she must have talked to you; even a dope-fiend that murders a little baby must have what

she calls some excuse for it, even a nigger dope-fiend
and a white baby —— or maybe even more, a nigger
dope-fiend and a white baby ——

GOWAN

I said, stop it, Boots.

He carries a tray containing a pitcher of water, a bowl of ice,
three empty tumblers and three whiskey glasses already filled.
The bottle itself protrudes from his topcoat pocket. He approaches Temple and offers the tray.

GOWAN

That's right. I'm going to have one myself. For a
change. After eight years. Why not?

TEMPLE

Why not?
    (looks at the tray)
Not highballs?

GOWAN

Not this one.

She takes one of the filled glasses. He offers the tray to Stevens,
who takes the second one. Then he sets the tray on the table
and takes up the third glass.

GOWAN

Nary a drink in eight years; count 'em. So maybe this
will be a good time to start again. At least, it wont be
too soon.
    (to Stevens)
Drink up. A little water behind it?

As though not aware that he had done so, he sets his untasted glass back on the tray, splashes water from the pitcher into a tumbler and hands the tumbler to Stevens as Stevens empties his glass and lowers it, taking the tumbler. Temple has not touched hers either.

GOWAN

Now maybe Defense Attorney Stevens will tell us what he wants here.

STEVENS

Your wife has already told you. To say goodbye.

GOWAN

Then say it. One more for the road, and where's your hat, huh?

He takes the tumbler from Stevens and turns back to the table.

TEMPLE (*sets her untasted glass back on the tray*)

And put ice in it this time, and maybe even a little water. But first, take Uncle Gavin's coat.

GOWAN (*takes bottle from his pocket and makes a highball for Stevens in the tumbler*)

That wont be necessary. If he could raise his arm in a white courtroom to defend a murdering nigger, he can certainly bend it in nothing but a wool overcoat—at least to take a drink with the victim's mother.

(*quickly: to Temple*)

Sorry. Maybe you were right all the time, and I was wrong. Maybe we've both got to keep on saying things like that until we can get rid of them, some of them, a little of them ——

TEMPLE

All right, why not. Here goes then.
> (*she is watching, not Gowan but Stevens, who*
> *watches her in return, grave and soberly*)

Dont forget the father too, dear.

GOWAN (*mixing the drink*)

Why should I, dear? How could I, dear? Except that
the child's father is unfortunately just a man. In the
eyes of the law, men are not supposed to suffer: they
are merely appellants or appellees. The law is tender
only of women and children—particularly of women,
particularly particular of nigger dope-fiend whores
who murder white children.

> (*hands the highball to Stevens, who takes it*)

So why should we expect Defense Attorney Stevens to
be tender of a man or a woman who just happen to be
the parents of the child that got murdered?

TEMPLE (*harshly*)

Will you for God's sake please get through? Then will
you for God's sake please hush?

GOWAN (*quickly: turns*)

Sorry.

> (*he turns toward her, sees her hand empty, then*
> *sees her full glass beside his own on the tray*)

No drink?

TEMPLE

I dont want it. I want some milk.

GOWAN

Right. Hot, of course.

TEMPLE

Please.

GOWAN (*turning*)

Right. I thought of that too. I put a pan on to heat
while I was getting the drinks.
(*crossing toward dining-room exit*)
Dont let Uncle Gavin get away until I get back. Lock
the door, if you have to. Or maybe just telephone that
nigger freedom agent—what's his name? ——

He exits. They dont move until the slap of the pantry door
sounds.

TEMPLE (*rapid and hard*)

How much do you know?
(*rapidly*)
Dont lie to me; dont you see there's not time?

STEVENS

Not time for what? Before your plane leaves tonight?
She has a little time yet—four months, until March,
the thirteenth of March ——

TEMPLE

You know what I mean—her lawyer—seeing her every
day—just a nigger, and you a white man—even if you
needed anything to frighten her with—you could just
buy it from her with a dose of cocaine or a pint of . . . . . .
(*she stops, stares at him, in a sort of amaze-
ment, despair; her voice is almost quiet*)

Oh, God, oh, God, she hasn't told you anything. It's me; I'm the one that's—— Dont you see? It's that I cannot believe—will not believe —— impossible ——

STEVENS

Impossible to believe that all human beings really dont—as you would put it—stink? Even—as you put it—dope-fiend nigger whores? No, she told me nothing more.

TEMPLE (*prompts*)

Even if there was anything more.

STEVENS

Even if there was.

TEMPLE

Then what is it you think you know? Never mind where you got it; just tell me what you think it is.

STEVENS

There was a man there that night.

TEMPLE (*quick, glib, almost before he has finished*)

Gowan.

STEVENS

That night? When Gowan had left with Bucky at six that morning to drive to New Orleans in a car?

TEMPLE (*quick, harsh*)

So I was right. Did you frighten her, or just buy it?
     (*interrupts herself*)

I'm trying. I'm really trying. Maybe it wouldn't be so
hard if I could just understand why they dont stink—
what reason they would have for not stinking . . . . . .
> (*she stops; it is as if she had heard a sound pre-*
> *saging Gowan's return, or perhaps simply knew*
> *by instinct or from knowledge of her own house,*
> *that he had had time to heat a cup of milk.*
> *Then continues, rapid and quiet*)

There was no man there. You see? I told you, warned
you, that you would get nothing from me. Oh, I know;
you could have put me on the stand at any time, under
oath; of course, your jury wouldn't have liked it—that
wanton crucifixion of a bereaved mamma, but what's
that in the balance with justice? I dont know why you
didn't. Or maybe you still intend to—provided you can
catch us before we cross the Tennessee line tonight.
> (*quick, tense, hard*)

All right. I'm sorry. I know better. So maybe it's just my
own stinking after all that I find impossible to doubt.
> (*the pantry door slaps again; they both hear it*)

Because I'm not even going to take Gowan with me
when I say goodbye and go up stairs.—And who
knows——

She stops. Gowan enters, carrying a small tray bearing a glass
of milk, a salt-shaker and a napkin, and comes to the table.

GOWAN
> What are you talking about now?

TEMPLE
> Nothing. I was telling Uncle Gavin that he had some-
> thing of Virginia or some sort of gentleman in him too

that he must have inherited from you through your grandfather, and that I'm going up to give Bucky his bath and supper.

> (*she touches the glass for heat, then takes it up:*
> *to Gowan*)

Thank you, dear.

GOWAN

Right, dear.

> (*to Stevens*)

You see? Not just a napkin: the right napkin. That's how I'm trained.

> (*he stops suddenly, noticing Temple, who has*
> *done nothing apparently: just standing there*
> *holding the milk. But he seems to know what is*
> *going on: to her*)

What's this for?

TEMPLE

I dont know.

He moves; they kiss, not long but not a peck either; definitely a kiss between a man and a woman. Then, carrying the milk, Temple crosses toward the hall door.

TEMPLE (*to Stevens*)

Goodbye then until next June. Bucky will send you and Maggie a postcard.

> (*she goes on to the door, pauses and looks back*
> *at Stevens*)

I may even be wrong about Temple Drake's odor too; if you should happen to hear something you haven't heard yet and it's true, I may even ratify it. Maybe you

can even believe that—if you can believe you are
going to hear anything that you haven't heard yet.

STEVENS

Do you?

TEMPLE (*after a moment*)

Not from me, Uncle Gavin. If someone wants to go to
heaven, who am I to stop them? Goodnight. Goodbye.

She exits, closes the door. Stevens, very grave, turns back and
sets his highball down on the tray.

GOWAN

Drink up. After all, I've got to eat supper and do some
packing too. How about it?

STEVENS

About what? the packing, or the drink? What about
you? I thought you were going to have one.

GOWAN

Oh, sure, sure.
(*takes up the small filled glass*)
Maybe you had better go on and leave us to our revenge.

STEVENS

I wish it could comfort you.

GOWAN

I wish to God it could. I wish to God that what I
wanted was only revenge. An eye for an eye—were

ever words emptier? Only, you have got to have lost
the eye to know it.

STEVENS

Yet she still has to die.

GOWAN

Why not? Even if she would be any loss—a nigger
whore, a drunkard, a dope-fiend——

STEVENS

—a vagabond, a tramp, hopeless until one day Mr and
Mrs Gowan Stevens out of simple pity and humanity
picked her up out of the gutter to give her one more
chance——
    (*Gowan stands motionless, his hand tightening
    slowly about the glass. Stevens watches him*)
And then in return for it——

GOWAN

Look, Uncle Gavin. Why dont you go for God's sake
home? Or to hell, or anywhere out of here?

STEVENS

I am, in a minute. Is that why you think—why you
would still say she has to die?

GOWAN

I dont. I had nothing to do with it. I wasn't even the
plaintiff. I didn't even instigate—that's the word, isn't
it?—the suit. My only connection with it was, I happened by chance to be the father of the child she——
Who in hell ever called that a drink?

He dashes the whiskey, glass and all, into the ice bowl, quickly catches up one of the empty tumblers in one hand and at the same time, tilts the whiskey bottle over it, pouring. At first he makes no sound, but at once it is obvious that he is laughing: laughter which begins normally enough, but almost immediately it is out of hand, just on hysteria, while he still pours whiskey into the glass, which in a moment now will overflow, except that Stevens reaches his hand and grasps the bottle and stops it.

STEVENS
Stop it. Stop it, now. Here.

He takes the bottle from Gowan, sets it down, takes the tumbler and tilts part of its contents into the other empty one, leaving at least a reasonable, a believable, drink, and hands it to Gowan. Gowan takes it, stopping the crazy laughter, gets hold of himself again.

GOWAN (*holding the glass untasted*)
Eight years. Eight years on the wagon—and this is what I got for it: my child murdered by a dope-fiend nigger whore that wouldn't even run so that a cop or somebody could have shot her down like the mad-dog—You see? Eight years without the drink, and so I got whatever it was I was buying by not drinking, and now I've got whatever it was I was paying for and it's paid for and so I can drink again. And now I dont want the drink. You see? Like whatever it was I was buying I not only didn't want, but what I was paying for it wasn't worth anything, wasn't even any loss. So I have a laugh coming. That's triumph. Because I got a bargain even in what I didn't want. I got a cut rate. I had two children. I had to pay only one of them to find out it wasn't

really costing me anything —— Half price: a child, and
a dope-fiend nigger whore on a public gallows: that's
all I had to pay for immunity.

STEVENS

There's no such thing.

GOWAN

From the past. From my folly. My drunkenness. My
cowardice, if you like ——

STEVENS

There's no such thing as past either.

GOWAN

That is a laugh, that one. Only, not so loud, huh? to
disturb the ladies—disturb Miss Drake—Miss Temple
Drake.—Sure, why not cowardice. Only, for euphony,
call it simple over-training. You know? Gowan
Stevens, trained at Virginia to drink like a gentleman,
gets drunk as ten gentlemen, takes a country college
girl, a maiden: who knows? maybe even a virgin, cross
country by car to another country college ball game,
gets drunker than twenty gentlemen, gets lost, gets still
drunker than forty gentlemen, wrecks the car, passes
eighty gentlemen now, passes completely out while
the maiden the virgin is being kidnapped into a Memphis whorehouse ——

(*he mumbles an indistinguishable word*)

STEVENS

What?

GOWAN

Sure; cowardice. Call it cowardice; what's a little euphony between old married people?

STEVENS

Not the marrying her afterward, at least. What——

GOWAN

Sure. Marrying her was purest Old Virginia. That was
indeed the hundred and sixty gentlemen.

STEVENS

The intent was, by any other standards too. The prisoner in the whorehouse; I didn't quite hear——

GOWAN (*quickly: reaching for it*)

Where's your glass? Dump that slop—— Here——

STEVENS (*holds glass*)

This will do. What was that you said about held prisoner in the whorehouse?

GOWAN (*harshly*)

That's all. You heard it.

STEVENS

You said 'and loved it'.
        (*they stare at each other*)
Is that what you can never forgive her for?—not for
having been the instrument creating that moment in
your life which you can never recall nor forget nor explain nor condone nor even stop thinking about, but
because she herself didn't even suffer, but on the con-

trary, even liked it—that month or whatever it was like
the episode in the old movie of the white girl held prisoner in the cave by the bedouin prince?—That you
had to lose not only your bachelor freedom, but your
man's self-respect in the chastity of his wife and your
child too, to pay for something your wife hadn't even
lost, didn't even regret, didn't even miss? Is that why
this poor lost doomed crazy Negro woman must die?

GOWAN (*tensely*)
Get out of here. Go on.

STEVENS
In a minute.—Or else, blow your own brains out: stop
having to remember, stop having to be forever unable
to forget: nothing; to plunge into nothing and sink and
drown forever and forever, never again to have to remember, never again to wake in the night writhing
and sweating because you cannot, can never not, stop
remembering? What else happened during that
month, that time while that madman held her prisoner there in that Memphis house, that nobody but
you and she know about, maybe not even you know
about?

Still staring at Stevens, slowly and deliberately Gowan sets the
glass of whiskey back on the tray and takes up the bottle and
swings it bottom up back over his head. The stopper is out, and
at once the whiskey begins to pour out of it, down his arm
and sleeve and onto the floor. He does not seem to be aware of
it even. His voice is tense, barely articulate.

GOWAN
So help me, Christ. . . . . . So help me, Christ.

A moment, then Stevens moves, without haste, sets his own glass back on the tray and turns, taking his hat as he passes the sofa, and goes on to the door and exits. Gowan stands a moment longer with the poised bottle, now empty. Then he draws a long shuddering breath, seems to rouse, wake, sets the empty bottle back on the tray, notices his untasted whiskey glass, takes it up, a moment: then turns and throws the glass crashing into the fireplace, against the burning gas logs, and stands, his back to the audience, and draws another long shuddering breath and then draws both hands hard down his face, then turns, looking at his wet sleeve, takes out his handkerchief and dabs at his sleeve as he comes back to the table, puts the handkerchief back in his pocket and takes the folded napkin from the small tray beside the salt cellar and wipes his sleeve with it, sees he is doing no good, tosses the crumpled napkin back onto the whiskey tray; and now, outwardly quite calm again, as though nothing had happened, he gathers the glasses back onto the big tray, puts the small tray and the napkin onto it too and takes up the tray and walks quietly toward the dining-room door as the lights begin to go down.

The lights go completely down. The stage is dark.

The lights go up.

SCENE III

Stevens living-room. 10:00 P.M. March eleventh.

The room is exactly as it was four months ago, except that the only light burning is the lamp on the table, and the sofa has been moved so that it partly faces the audience, with a small motionless blanket-wrapped object lying on it, and one of the chairs placed between the lamp and the sofa so that the shadow of its back falls across the object on the sofa, making it more or less indistinguishable, and the dining-room doors are now closed. The telephone sits on the small stand in the corner R as in scene 2.

The hall door opens. Temple enters, followed by Stevens. She now wears a long housecoat; her hair is tied back with a ribbon as though prepared for bed. This time Stevens carries the topcoat and the hat too; his suit is different. Apparently she has already warned Stevens to be quiet; his air anyway shows it. She enters, stops, lets him pass her. He pauses, looks about the room, sees the sofa, stands looking at it.

STEVENS
　　This is what they call a plant.

He crosses to the sofa, Temple watching him, and stops, looking down at the shadowed object. He quietly draws aside the shadowing chair and reveals a little boy, about four, wrapped in the blanket, asleep.

TEMPLE
　　Why not? Dont the philosophers and other gynecologists tell us that women will strike back with any weapon, even their children?

STEVENS (*watching the child*)
　　Including the sleeping pill you told me you gave Gowan?

TEMPLE
　　All right.
　　　　(*approaches table*)

If I would just stop struggling: how much time we could
save. I came all the way back from California, but I still
cant seem to quit. Do you believe in coincidence?

STEVENS (*turns*)
    Not unless I have to.

TEMPLE (*at table, takes up a folded yellow telegraph form,
            opens it, reads*)
    Dated Jefferson, March sixth. 'You have a week yet
    until the thirteenth. But where will you go then?'
    signed Gavin.

She folds the paper back into its old creases, folds it still again.
Stevens watches her.

STEVENS
    Well? This is the eleventh. Is that the coincidence?

TEMPLE
    No. This is.
        (*she drops, tosses the folded paper onto the
        table, turns*)
    It was that afternoon—the sixth. We were on the
    beach, Bucky and I. I was reading, and he was—oh,
    talking mostly, you know—'Is California far from Jef-
    ferson, mamma?' and I say 'Yes, darling'—you know:
    still reading or trying to, and he says, 'How long will we
    stay in California, mamma?' and I say, 'Until we get
    tired of it' and he says, 'Will we stay here until they
    hang Nancy, mamma?' and it's already too late then; I
    should have seen it coming but it's too late now; I say,
    'Yes, darling' and then he drops it right in my lap, right
    out of the mouths of—how is it?—babes and suck-

lings? 'Where will we go then, mamma?' And then we
come back to the hotel, and there you are too. Well?

STEVENS
    Well what?

TEMPLE
    All right. Let's for God's sake stop.
        (*goes to a chair*)
    Now that I'm here, no matter whose fault it was, what
    do you want? A drink? Will you drink? At least, put
    your coat and hat down.

STEVENS
    I dont even know yet. That's why you came back——

TEMPLE (*interrupts*)
    I came back? It wasn't I who——

STEVENS (*interrupts*)
    —who said, let's for God's sake stop.

They stare at each other: a moment.

TEMPLE
    All right. Put down your coat and hat.

Stevens lays his hat and coat on a chair. Temple sits down.
Stevens takes a chair opposite, so that the sleeping child on the
sofa is between them in background.

TEMPLE
    So Nancy must be saved. So you send for me, or
    you and Bucky between you, or anyway here you are

and here I am. Because apparently I know something
I haven't told yet, or maybe you know something I
haven't told yet. What do you think you know?
(*quickly; he says nothing*)
All right. What do you know?

STEVENS
Nothing. I dont want to know it. All I ——

TEMPLE
Say that again.

STEVENS
Say what again?

TEMPLE
What is it you think you know?

STEVENS
Nothing. I ——

TEMPLE
All right. Why do you think there is something I
haven't told yet?

STEVENS
You came back. All the way from California ——

TEMPLE
Not enough. Try again.

STEVENS
You were there.

*(with her face averted, Temple reaches her hand
to the table, fumbles until she finds the cigarette box, takes a cigarette and with the same
hand fumbles until she finds the lighter, draws
them back to her lap)*

At the trial. Every day. All day, from the time court
opened——

TEMPLE *(still not looking at him, supremely casual, puts
the cigarette into her mouth, talking around it, the
cigarette bobbing)*

The bereaved mother——

STEVENS

Yes, the bereaved mother——

TEMPLE *(the cigarette bobbing: still not looking at him)*
——herself watching the accomplishment of her revenge; the tigress over the body of her slain cub——

STEVENS

—who should have been too immersed in grief to have
thought of revenge—to have borne the very sight of
her child's murderer. . . .

TEMPLE *(not looking at him)*

Methinks she doth protest too much?

Stevens doesn't answer. She snaps the lighter on, lights the cigarette, puts the lighter back on the table. Leaning, Stevens
pushes the ashtray along the table until she can reach it. Now
she looks at him.

TEMPLE

> Thanks. Now let grandmamma teach you how to suck
> an egg. It doesn't matter what I know, what you think I
> know, what might have happened. Because we wont
> even need it. All we need is an affidavit. That she is
> crazy. Has been for years.

STEVENS

> I thought of that too. Only it's too late. That should
> have been done about five months ago. The trial is
> over now. She has been convicted and sentenced. In
> the eyes of the law, she is already dead. In the eyes of
> the law, Nancy Mannigoe doesn't even exist. Even if
> there wasn't a better reason than that. The best reason
> of all.

TEMPLE (*smoking*)

> Yes?

STEVENS

> We haven't got one.

TEMPLE (*smoking*)

> Yes?
>
>> (*she sits back in the chair, smoking rapidly,
>> looking at Stevens. Her voice is gentle, patient,
>> only a little too rapid, like the smoking*)
>
> That's right. Try to listen. Really try. I am the affidavit;
> what else are we doing here at ten oclock at night
> barely a day from her execution? What else did I—as
> you put it—come all the way back from California for,
> not to mention a—as you have probably put that too—
> faked coincidence to save—as I would put it I sup-

pose — my face? All we need now is to decide just how much of what to put in the affidavit. Do try; maybe you had better have a drink after all.

STEVENS

Later, maybe. I'm dizzy enough right now with just perjury and contempt of court.

TEMPLE

What perjury?

STEVENS

Not venal then, worse: inept. After my client is not only convicted but sentenced, I turn up with the prosecution's chief witness offering evidence to set the whole trial aside ——

TEMPLE

Tell them I forgot this. Or tell them I changed my mind. Tell them the district attorney bribed me to keep my mouth shut——

STEVENS (*peremptory yet quiet*)
Temple.

She puffs rapidly at the cigarette, removes it from her mouth.

TEMPLE

Or better still; wont it be obvious? a woman whose child was smothered in its crib, wanting vengeance, capable of anything to get the vengeance; then when she has it, realising she cant go through with it, cant sacrifice a human life for it, even a nigger whore's?

STEVENS

> Stop it. One at a time. At least, let's talk about the same thing.

TEMPLE

> What else are we talking about except saving a condemned client whose trained lawyer has already admitted that he has failed?

STEVENS

> Then you really dont want her to die. You did invent the coincidence.

TEMPLE

> Didn't I just say so? At least, let's for God's sake stop that, cant we?

STEVENS

> Done. So Temple Drake will have to save her.

TEMPLE

> Mrs Gowan Stevens will.

STEVENS

> Temple Drake.

She stares at him, smoking, deliberately now. Deliberately she removes the cigarette and, still watching him, reaches and snubs it out in the ashtray.

STEVENS

> All right. Tell me again. Maybe I'll even understand this time, let alone listen. We produce—turn up

with—a sworn affidavit that this murdress was crazy
when she committed the crime.

TEMPLE

You did listen, didn't you? Who knows——

STEVENS

Based on what?

TEMPLE

——What?

STEVENS

The affidavit. Based on what?
          (*she stares at him*)
On what proof?

TEMPLE

Proof?

STEVENS

Proof. What will be in the affidavit? What are we going
to affirm now that for some reason, any reason, we—
you—we didn't see fit to bring up or anyway didn't
bring up until after she ——

TEMPLE

How do I know? You're the lawyer. What do you want
in it? What do such affidavits have in them, need to
have in them, to make them work, make them sure to
work? Dont you have samples in your law books—
reports, whatever you call them—that you can copy
and have me swear to? Good ones, certain ones? At

least, while we're committing whatever this is, pick out
a good one, such a good one that nobody, not even an
untrained lawyer, can punch holes in it . . . . .

Her voice ceases. She stares at him, while he continues to look
steadily back at her, saying nothing, just looking at her, until at
last she draws a loud harsh breath; her voice is harsh too.

TEMPLE
    What do you want then? What more do you want?

STEVENS
    Temple Drake.

TEMPLE (*quick, harsh, immediate*)
    No. Mrs Gowan Stevens.

STEVENS (*implacable and calm*)
    Temple Drake. The truth.

TEMPLE
    Truth? We're trying to save a condemned murdress
    whose lawyer has already admitted that he has failed.
    What has truth got to do with that?
        (*rapid, harsh*)
    We? I, I, the mother of the baby she murdered; not
    you, Gavin Stevens, the lawyer, but I, Mrs Gowan
    Stevens, the mother. Cant you get it through your
    head that I will do anything, *any*thing?

STEVENS
    Except one. Which is all. We're not concerned with
    death. That's nothing: any handful of petty facts and

sworn documents can cope with that. That's all finished now; we can forget it. What we are trying to deal
with now is injustice. Only truth can cope with that.
Or love.

TEMPLE (*harshly*)
Love. Oh, God. Love.

STEVENS
Call it pity then. Or courage. Or simple honor, hon-
esty, or a simple desire for the right to sleep at night.

TEMPLE
You prate of sleep, to me, who learned six years ago
how not even to realise anymore that I didn't mind not
sleeping at night?

STEVENS
Yet you invented the coincidence.

TEMPLE
Will you for Christ's sake stop? Will you . . . . . All
right. Then if her dying is nothing, what do you want?
What in God's name do you want?

STEVENS
I told you. Truth.

TEMPLE
And I told you that what you keep on harping at as
truth, has nothing to do with this. When you go before
the—What do you call this next collection of trained
lawyers? supreme court?—what you will need will be

facts, papers, documents, sworn to, incontrovertible, that no other lawyer trained or untrained either can punch holes in, find any flaw in.

STEVENS

We're not going to the supreme court.

(*she stares at him*)

That's all finished. If that could have been done, would have sufficed, I would have thought of that, attended to that, four months ago. We're going to the governor. Tonight.

TEMPLE

The governor?

STEVENS

Perhaps he wont save her either. He probably wont.

TEMPLE

Then why ask him? Why?

STEVENS

I've told you. Truth.

TEMPLE (*in quiet amazement*)

For no more than that. For no better reason than that. Just to get it told, breathed aloud, into words, sound. Just to be heard by, told to, someone, anyone, any stranger none of whose business it is, can possibly be, simply because he is capable of hearing, comprehending it. Why blink your own rhetoric? Why dont you go on and tell me it's for the good of my soul—if I have one?

STEVENS

I did. I said, so you can sleep at night.

TEMPLE

And I told you I forgot six years ago even what it was to
miss the sleep.

She stares at him. He doesn't answer, looking at her. Still
watching him, she reaches her hand to the table, toward the
cigarette box, then stops, is motionless, her hand suspended,
staring at him.

TEMPLE

There is something else, then. We're even going to get
the true one this time. All right. Shoot.

He doesn't answer, makes no sign, watching her. A moment:
then she turns her head and looks toward the sofa and the sleeping child. Still looking at the child, she rises and crosses to the
sofa and stands looking down at the child; her voice is quiet.

TEMPLE

So it was a plant, after all; I just didn't seem to know for
who.
        (she looks down at the child)
I threw my remaining child at you. Now you threw
him back.

STEVENS

But I didn't wake him.

TEMPLE

Then I've got you, lawyer. What would be better for his
peace and sleep than to hang his sister's murderer?

STEVENS
No matter by what means, in what lie?

TEMPLE
Nor whose.

STEVENS
Yet you invented the coincidence.

TEMPLE
Mrs Gowan Stevens did.

STEVENS
Temple Drake did. Mrs Gowan Stevens is not even
fighting in this class. This is Temple Drake's.

TEMPLE
Temple Drake is dead.

STEVENS
The past is never dead. It's not even past.

She comes back to the table, takes a cigarette from the box,
puts it in her mouth and reaches for the lighter. He leans as
though to hand it to her, but she has already found it, snaps it
on and lights the cigarette, talking through the smoke.

TEMPLE
Listen. How much do you know?

STEVENS
Nothing.

TEMPLE
Swear.

STEVENS
  Would you believe me?

TEMPLE
  No. But swear anyway.

STEVENS
  All right. I swear.

TEMPLE (*crushes cigarette into tray*)
  Then listen. Listen carefully.
      (*she stands, tense, rigid, facing him, staring at
      him*)
  Temple Drake is dead. Temple Drake will have been
  dead six years longer than Nancy Mannigoe will ever
  be. If all Nancy Mannigoe has to save her is Temple
  Drake, then God help Nancy Mannigoe. Now get out
  of here.

She stares at him; another moment. Then he rises, still watching her; she stares steadily and implacably back. Then he moves.

TEMPLE
  Goodnight.

STEVENS
  Goodnight.

He goes back to the chair, takes up his coat and hat, then goes on to the hall door, has put his hand on the knob.

TEMPLE
  Gavin.

(*he pauses, his hand on the knob, and looks
back at her*)

Maybe I'll have the handkerchief, after all.

(*he looks at her a moment longer, then releases
the knob, takes the handkerchief from his breast
pocket as he crosses back toward her, extends it.
She doesn't take it*)

All right. What will I have to do? What do you suggest,
then?

STEVENS

Everything.

TEMPLE

Which of course I wont. I will not. You can understand that, cant you? At least you can hear it. So let's
start over, shall we? How much will I have to tell?

STEVENS

Everything.

TEMPLE

Then I wont need the handkerchief, after all. Goodnight. Close the front door when you go out, please.
It's getting cold again.

He turns, crosses again to the door without stopping nor looking back, exits, closes the door behind him. She is not watching him either now. For a moment after the door has closed,
she doesn't move. Then she makes a gesture something like
Gowan's in scene 2, except that she merely presses her palms
for a moment hard against her face, her face calm, expression-
less, cold, drops her hands, turns, picks up the crushed cigarette from beside the tray and puts it into the tray and takes up

the tray and crosses to the fireplace, glancing down at the
sleeping child as she passes the sofa, empties the tray into the
fireplace and returns to the table and puts the tray on it and
this time pauses at the sofa and stoops and tucks the blanket
closer about the sleeping child and then goes on to the telephone and lifts the receiver.

TEMPLE (*into the phone*)
      Two three nine, please.
            (*while she stands waiting for the answer, there
            is a slight movement in the darkness beyond the
            open door at rear, just enough silent movement
            to show that something or someone is there or
            has moved there. Temple is unaware of it since
            her back is turned. Then she speaks into the
            phone*)
      Maggie? Temple. . . . Yes, suddenly . . . Oh, I dont
      know; perhaps we got bored with sunshine. . . . Of
      course, I may drop in tomorrow. I wanted to leave a
      message for Gavin . . . I know; he just left here. Some-
      thing I forgot . . . If you'll ask him to call me when he
      comes in . . . . Yes . . . . Wasn't it. . . . . Yes . . . . If
      you will . . . Thank you.
            (*she puts the receiver down and starts to turn
            back into the room when the telephone rings.
            She turns back, takes up the receiver, speaks
            into it*)
      Hello . . . Yes. Coincidence again; I had my hand on
      it; I had just called Maggie . . . . Oh, the filling station.
      I didn't think you had had time. I can be ready in thirty
      minutes. Your car, or ours? . . . All right. Listen . . .
      Yes, I'm here. Gavin . . . How much will I have to
      tell?
            (*hurriedly*)

Oh, I know: you've already told me eight or ten times.
But maybe I didn't hear it right. How much will I have
to tell?

> (*she listens a moment, quiet, frozen-faced, then
> slowly begins to lower the receiver toward the
> stand; she speaks quietly, without inflection*)

Oh, God. Oh, God.

> (*she puts the receiver down, crosses to the sofa,
> snaps off the table lamp and takes up the child
> and crosses to the door to the hall, snaps off the
> remaining room lights as she goes out, so that
> the only light in the room now enters from the
> hall. As soon as she has disappeared from sight,
> Gowan enters from the door at rear, dressed ex-
> cept for his coat, vest and tie. He has obviously
> taken no sleeping pill. He goes to the phone
> and stands quietly beside it, facing the hall
> door and obviously listening until Temple is
> safely away. Now the hall light snaps off, and
> the stage is in complete darkness*)

GOWAN'S VOICE (*quietly*)

Two three nine, please . . . Good evening, Aunt Maggie. Gowan . . . All right, thank you . . . Sure, some-
time tomorrow. As soon as Uncle Gavin comes in, will
you have him call me? I'll be right here. Thank you.

> (*sound of the receiver as he puts it back*)

(*Curtain*)

ACT II

The Golden Dome

(BEGINNING WAS τὸ ἔυ)

Jackson. Alt. 294 ft. Pop. (A.D. 1950) 201,092.
Located by an expedition of three Commissioners selected appointed and dispatched for that single purpose, on a high bluff above Pearl River at the approximate geographical center of the State, to be not a market nor industrial town, nor even as a place for men to live, but to be a capital, the Capital of a Commonwealth;

In the beginning was already decreed this rounded knob, this gilded pustule, already before and beyond the steamy chiaroscuro, untimed unseasoned winterless miasma not any one of water or earth or life yet all of each, inextricable and indivisible; that one seethe one spawn one mother-womb, one furious tumescence, father-mother-one, one vast incubant ejaculation already fissionating in one boiling moil of litter from the celestial experimental Work Bench; that one spawning crawl and creep printing with three-toed mastodonic tracks the steamy-green swaddling clothes of the coal and the oil, above which the pea-brained reptilian heads curved the heavy leather-flapped air;

Then the ice, but still this knob, this pimple-dome, this buried half-ball hemisphere; the earth lurched, heaving darkward the

[79]

long continental flank, dragging upward beneath the polar cap
that furious equatorial womb, the shutter-lid of cold severing
off into blank and heedless void one last sound, one cry, one
puny myriad indictment already fading and then no more, the
blind and tongueless earth spinning on, looping the long
recordless astral orbit, frozen, tideless, yet still was there this
tiny gleam, this spark, this gilded crumb of man's eternal aspiration, this golden dome preordained and impregnable, this
minuscule foetus-glint tougher than ice and harder than
freeze; the earth lurched again, sloughing; the ice with infinitesimal speed, scouring out the valleys, scoring the hills, and
vanished; the earth tilted further to recede the sea rim by
necklace-rim of crustacean husks in recessional contour lines
like the concentric whorls within the sawn stump telling the
tree's age, baring south by recessional south toward that mute
and beckoning gleam the confluent continental swale, baring
to light and air the broad blank mid-continental page for the
first scratch of orderly recording—a laboratory-factory covering
what would be twenty states, established and ordained for the
purpose of manufacturing one: the ordered unhurried whirl of
seasons, of rain and snow and freeze and thaw and sun and
drouth to aereate and slack the soil, the conflux of a hundred
rivers into one vast father of rivers carrying the rich dirt, the
rich garnering, south and south, carving the bluffs to bear the
long march of the river towns, flooding the Mississippi low-
lands, spawning the rich alluvial dirt layer by vernal layer, raising inch by foot by year by century the surface of the earth
which in time (not distant now, measured against that long sig-
natureless chronicle) would tremble to the passing of trains
like when the cat crosses the suspension bridge;

The rich deep black alluvial soil which would grow cotton
taller than the head of a man on a horse, already one jungle

one brake one impassable density of brier and cane and vine
interlocking the soar of gum and cypress and hickory and
pinoak and ash, printed now by the tracks of unalien shapes—
bear and deer and panthers and bison and wolves and alligators
and the myriad smaller beasts, and unalien men to name them
too perhaps—the (themselves) nameless though recorded pre-
decessors who built the mounds to escape the spring floods
and left their meagre artifacts: the obsolete and the dispossessed, dispossessed by those who were dispossessed in turn because they too were obsolete: the wild Algonquian, Chickasaw
and Choctaw and Natchez and Pascagoula, peering in virgin
astonishment down from the tall bluffs at a Chippeway canoe
bearing three Frenchmen—and had barely time to whirl and
look behind him at ten and then a hundred and then a thousand Spaniards come overland from the Atlantic Ocean: a tide,
a wash, a thrice flux-and-ebb of motion so rapid and quick
across the land's slow alluvial chronicle as to resemble the
limber flicking of the magician's one hand before the other
holding the deck of inconstant cards: the Frenchman for a moment, then the Spaniard for perhaps two, then the Frenchman
for another two and then the Spaniard again for another and
then the Frenchman for that one last second, half-breath; because then came the Anglo-Saxon, the pioneer, the tall man,
roaring with Protestant scripture and boiled whiskey, Bible and
jug in one hand and (like as not) a native tomahawk in the
other, brawling, turbulent not through viciousness but simply
because of his over-revved glands; uxorious and polygamous: a
married invincible bachelor, dragging his gravid wife and most
of the rest of his mother-in-law's family behind him into the
trackless infested forest, spawning that child as like as not behind the barricade of a rifle-crotched log mapless leagues from
nowhere and then getting her with another one before reaching his final itch-footed destination, and at the same time scat-

tering his ebullient seed in a hundred dusky bellies through a thousand miles of wilderness; innocent and gullible, without bowels for avarice or compassion or forethought either, changing the face of the earth: felling a tree which took two hundred years to grow, in order to extract from it a bear or a capful of wild honey;

Obsolete too: still felling the two-hundred-year-old tree when the bear and the wild honey were gone and there was nothing in it anymore but a raccoon or a possum whose hide was worth at the most two dollars, turning the earth into a howling waste from which he would be the first to vanish, not even on the heels but synchronous with the slightly darker wild men whom he had dispossessed, because, like them, only the wilderness could feed and nourish him; and so disappeared, strutted his roaring eupeptic hour, and was no more, leaving his ghost, pariah and proscribed, scriptureless now and armed only with the highwayman's, the murderer's, pistol, haunting the fringes of the wilderness which he himself had helped to destroy, because the river towns marched now recessional south by south along the processional bluffs: St Louis, Paducah, Memphis, Helena, Vicksburg, Natchez, Baton Rouge, peopled by men with mouths full of law, in broadcloth and flowered waistcoats, who owned Negro slaves and Empire beds and buhl cabinets and ormolu clocks, who strolled and smoked their cigars along the bluffs beneath which in the shanty and flatboat purlieus he rioted out the last of his doomed evening, losing his worthless life again and again to the fierce knives of his drunken and worthless kind;—this in the intervals of being pursued and harried in his vanishing avatars of Harpe and Hare and Mason and Murrel, either shot on sight or hoicked, dragged out of what remained of his secret wilderness haunts along the overland Natchez Trace (one day someone brought a curious seed into the land and inserted it into the

earth, and now vast fields of white not only covered the waste
places which with his wanton and heedless axe he had made,
but were effacing, thrusting back the wilderness even faster than
he had been able to, so that he barely had a screen for his back
when, crouched in his thicket, he glared at his dispossessor in
impotent and incredulous and uncomprehending rage) into the
towns to his formal apotheosis in a courtroom and then a gallows
or the limb of a tree;

Because those days were gone, the old brave innocent tumul-
tuous eupeptic tomorrowless days; the last broadhorn and keel-
boat (Mike Fink was a legend; soon even the grandfathers would
no longer claim to remember him, and the river hero was now
the steamboat gambler wading ashore in his draggled finery
from the towhead where the captain had marooned him) had
been sold piecemeal for firewood in Chartres and Toulouse and
Dauphine street, and Choctaw and Chickasaw braves, in short
hair and overalls and armed with mule-whips in place of war-
clubs and already packed up to move west to Oklahoma,
watched steamboats furrowing even the shallowest and remotest
wilderness streams where tumbled gently to the motion of the
paddle-wheels, the gutted rock-weighted bones of Hare's and
Mason's murderees; a new time, a new age, millennium's beginning; one vast single net of commerce webbed and veined
the mid-continent's fluvial embracement; New Orleans, Pittsburgh, and Fort Bridger, Wyoming, were suburbs one to the
other, inextricable in destiny; men's mouths were full of law and
order, all men's mouths were round with the sound of money;
one unanimous golden affirmation ululated the nation's boundless immeasurable forenoon: profit plus regimen equals security:
a nation of commonwealths; that crumb, that dome, that gilded
pustule, that Idea risen now, suspended like a balloon or a portent or a thundercloud above what used to be wilderness, draw-

ing, holding the eyes of all: Mississippi: a state, a commonwealth; triumvirate in legislative, judiciary, executive, but without a capital, functioning as though from a field headquarters,
operating as though still en route toward that high inevitable
place in the galaxy of commonwealths, so in 1820 from its field
p.c. at Columbia the legislature selected appointed and dispatched the three Commissioners Hinds Lattimore and Patton,
not three politicians and less than any three political timeservers
but soldiers engineers and patriots—soldier to cope with the reality, engineer to cope with the aspiration, patriot to hold fast to
the dream—three white men in a Choctaw pirogue moving
slowly up the empty reaches of a wilderness river as two centuries ago the three Frenchmen had drifted in their Northern
birchbark down that vaster and emptier one;

But not drifting, these: paddling: because this was upstream,
bearing not volitionless into the unknown mystery and authority, but establishing in the wilderness a point for men to rally to
in conscience and free will, scanning, watching the dense inscrutable banks in their turn too, conscious of the alien incor-
rigible eyes too perhaps but already rejectant of them, not that
the wilderness's dark denizens, already dispossessed at Doak's
Stand, were less inveterate now, but because this canoe bore
not the meek and bloody cross of Christ and Saint Louis, but
the scales the blindfold and the sword,—up the river to Le
Fleur's Bluff, the trading-post store on the high mild promon-
tory established by the Canadian *voyageur*, whose name, called
and spelled 'Leflore' now, would be borne by the half-French
half-Choctaw hereditary first chief of the Choctaw nation who,
siding with the white men at the Council of Dancing Rabbit,
would remain in Mississippi after his people departed for the
west, to become in time among the first of the great slave-
holding cotton planters and leave behind him a county and its

seat named for himself and a plantation named in honor of a
French king's mistress,—stopping at last though still paddling
slowly to hold the pirogue against the current, looking not up
at the dark dispossessed faces watching them from the top of
the bluff, but looking staring rather from one to another
among themselves in the transfixed boat, saying, 'This is the
city. This is the State';

1821, General Hinds and his co-commissioners, with Abraham
DeFrance, superintendent of public buildings at Washington,
to advise them, laid out the city according to Thomas Jefferson's plan to Territorial Governor Claiborne seventeen years
ago, and built the statehouse, thirty by forty feet of brick and
clay and native limestone yet large enough to contain the
dream; the first legislature convened in it in the new year 1822;

And named the city after the other old hero, hero Hinds'
brother-in-arms on beaten British and Seminole fields and
presently to be President—the old duellist, the brawling lean
fierce mangy durable old lion who set the well-being of the Nation above the White House, and the health of his new political party above either, and above them all set, not his wife's
honor, but the principle that honor must be defended whether
it was or not since, defended, it was, whether or not;—Jackson,
that the new city created not for a city but a central point for
the governance of men, might partake of the successful soldier's courage and endurance and luck, and named the area
surrounding it 'Hinds County' after the lesser hero, as the
hero's quarters, even empty, not only partake of his dignity but
even guard and increase its stature;

And needed them, the luck at least: in 1829 the Senate passed
a bill authorising the removal of the capital to Clinton, the

House defeated it; in 1830 the House itself voted to move to
Port Gibson on the Mississippi, but with the next breath re-
considered, reneged, the following day they voted to move to
Vicksburg but nothing came of that either, no records (Sherman burned them in 1863 and notified his superior, General
Grant, by note of hand with comfortable and encouraging
brevity.) to show just what happened this time: a trial, a dry run
perhaps or perhaps still enchannelled by a week's or a month's
rut of habit or perhaps innocent in juvenility, absent or anyway
missing the unanimous voice or presence of the three patriot-
dreamers who forced the current and bore the dream, like a
child with dynamite: innocent of its own power for alteration:
until in 1832, perhaps in simple self-defense or perhaps in simple weariness, a constitution was written designating Jackson as
the capital if not in perpetuity at least in escrow until 1850,
when (hoped perhaps) a maturer legislature would be composed of maturer men outgrown or anyway become used to the
novelty of manipulation;

Which by that time was enough; Jackson was secure, impregnable to simple toyment; fixed and founded strong, it would
endure always; men had come there to live and the railroads
had followed them, crossing off with steel cancellations the age
of the steamboat: in '36 to Vicksburg, in '37 to Natchez, then
last of all the junction of two giving a route from New Orleans
to Tennessee and the Southern railroad to New York and the
Atlantic Ocean; secure and fixed: in 1836 Old Hickory himself
addressed the legislature in its own halls, five years later Henry
Clay was entertained under that roof; it knew the convention
called to consider Clay's last compromise, it saw that Convention in 1861 which declared Mississippi to be the third star in
that new galaxy of commonwealths dedicated to the principle
that voluntary communities of men shall be not just safe but

even secured from Federal meddling, and knew General Pemberton while defending that principle and right, and Joseph Johnston: and Sherman: and fire: and nothing remained, a City of Chimneys (once pigs rooted in the streets; now rats did) ruled over by a general of the United States army while the new blood poured in: men who had followed, pressed close the Federal field armies with spoiled grain and tainted meat and spavined mules, now pressing close the Federal provost-marshals with carpet bags stuffed with blank ballot-forms on which freed slaves could mark their formal X's;

But endured; the government, which fled before Sherman in 1863, returned in '65, and even grew too despite the fact that a city government of carpet-baggers held on long after the State as a whole had dispossessed them; in 1869 Tougaloo College for Negroes was founded, in 1884 Jackson College for Negroes was brought from Natchez, in 1898 Campbell College for Negroes removed from Vicksburg; Negro leaders developed by these schools intervened when in 1868 one 'Buzzard' Egglestone instigated the use of troops to drive Governor Humphries from the executive offices and mansion; in 1887 Jackson women sponsored the Kermis Ball lasting three days to raise money for a monument to the Confederate dead; in 1884 Jefferson Davis spoke for his last time in public at the old Capitol; in 1890 the state's greatest convention drew up the present constitution;

And still the people and the railroads: the New Orleans and Great Northern down the Pearl River valley, the Gulf Mobile and Northern northeast; Alabama and the eastern black prairies were almost a commuter's leap and a line to Yazoo City and the upper river towns made of the Great Lakes five suburban ponds; the Gulf and Ship Island opened the south

Mississippi lumber boom and Chicago voices spoke among
the magnolias and the odor of jasmine and oleander; population doubled and trebled in a decade, in 1892 Millsaps College
opened its doors to assume its place among the first establish-
ments for higher learning; then the natural gas and the oil,
Texas and Oklahoma license plates flitted like a migration of
birds about the land and the tall flames from the vent-pipes
stood like incandescent plumes above the century-cold ashes
of Choctaw camp-fires and the vanished imprints of deer; and
in 1903 the new Capitol was completed—the golden dome,
the knob, the gleamy crumb, the gilded pustule longer than
the miasma and the gigantic ephemeral saurians, more
durable than the ice and the pre-night cold, soaring, hanging
as one blinding spheroid above the center of the Commonwealth, incapable of being either looked full or evaded,
peremptory, irrefragible, and reassuring;

In the roster of Mississippi names:
Claiborne. Humphries. Dickson. McLaurin. Barksdale. Lamar.
Prentiss. Davis. Sartoris. Compson;

In the roster of cities:
JACKSON. Alt. 294 ft. Pop. (A.D. 1950) 201,092
Railroads: Illinois Central, Yazoo & Mississippi Valley, Ala-
     bama & Vicksburg, Gulf & Ship Island.
Bus: Tri-State Transit, Varnado, Thomas, Greyhound, Dixie-
     Greyhound, Teche-Greyhound, Oliver.
Air: Delta, Chicago & Southern.
Transport: Street busses, Taxis.
Accommodations: Hotels, Tourist camps, Rooming houses.
Radio: WJDX, WTJS.
Diversions: chronic: S.I.A.A. Basketball Tournament, Music
     Festival, Junior Auxiliary Follies, May Day Festival, State

Tennis Tournament, Red Cross Water Pageant, State Fair, Junior Auxiliary Style Show, Girl Scouts Horseshow, Feast of Carols.

Diversions: acute: Religion, Politics.

SCENE I

Office of the Governor of the State. 2:00 A.M. March twelfth.

The whole bottom of the stage is in darkness, as in Scene 1, Act I, so that the visible scene has the effect of being held in the beam of a spotlight. Suspended too, since it is upper L and even higher above the shadow of the stage proper than the same in Scene 1, Act I, carrying still further the symbolism of the still higher, the last, the ultimate seat of judgment.

It is a corner or section of the office of the Governor of the Commonwealth, late at night, about two a.m.—a clock on the wall says two minutes past two—, a massive flat-topped desk bare except for an ashtray and a telephone, behind it a high-backed heavy chair like a throne; on the wall behind and above the chair, is the emblem, official badge, of the State, sovereignty (a mythical one, since this is rather the State of which Yoknapatawpha County is a unit)—an eagle, the blind scales of justice, a device in Latin perhaps, against a flag. There are two other chairs in front of the desk, turned slightly to face each other, the length of the desk between them.

The Governor stands in front of the high chair, between it and the desk, beneath the emblem on the wall. He is symbolic too: no known person, neither old nor young; he might be someone's idea not of God but of Gabriel perhaps, the Gabriel not before the Crucifixion but after it. He has obviously just been routed out of bed or at least out of his study or dressing-room; he wears a dressing gown, though there is a collar and tie beneath it, and his hair is neatly combed.

Temple and Stevens have just entered. Temple wears the same fur coat, hat, bag, gloves etc. as in Act I, Scene 2, Stevens is dressed exactly as he was in Scene 3, Act I, is carrying his hat. They are moving toward the two chairs at either end of the desk.

STEVENS
    Good morning, Henry. Here we are.

GOVERNOR
    Yes. Sit down.
        (*as Temple sits down*)
    Does Mrs Stevens smoke?

STEVENS
    Yes. Thank you.

He takes a pack of cigarettes from his topcoat pocket, as though he had come prepared for the need, emergency. He works one of them free and extends the pack to Temple. The Governor puts one hand into his dressing gown pocket and withdraws it, holding something in his closed fist.

TEMPLE (*takes the cigarette*)
    What, no blindfold?
        (*the Governor extends his hand across the desk.
        It contains a lighter. Temple puts the cigarette*

    into her mouth. The Governor snaps on the
    lighter)
But of course, the only one waiting execution is back
there in Jefferson. So all we need to do here is, fire
away, and hope that at least the volley rids us of the
metaphor.

GOVERNOR
    Metaphor?

TEMPLE
    The blindfold. The firing squad. Or is metaphor
    wrong? Or maybe it's the joke. But dont apologise; a
    joke that has to be diagrammed is like trying to excuse
    an egg, isn't it? The only thing you can do is, bury
    them both, quick.
        (the Governor approaches the flame to Tem-
        ple's cigarette. She leans and accepts the light,
        then sits back)
    Thanks.

The Governor closes the lighter, sits down in the tall chair behind the desk, still holding the lighter in his hand, his hands
resting on the desk before him. Stevens sits down in the other
chair across from Temple, laying the pack of cigarettes on the
desk beside him.

GOVERNOR
    What has Mrs Gowan Stevens to tell me?

TEMPLE
    Not tell you: ask you. No, that's wrong. I could have
    asked you to revoke or commute or whatever you do to

a sentence to hang when we—Uncle Gavin tele-
phoned you last night.

(*to Stevens*)

Go on. Tell him. Aren't you the mouthpiece?—isn't
that how you say it? Dont lawyers always tell their
patients—I mean clients—never to say anything at all:
to let them do all the talking?

GOVERNOR

That's only before the client enters the witness stand.

TEMPLE

So this is the witness stand.

GOVERNOR

You have come all the way here from Jefferson at two
oclock in the morning. What would you call it?

TEMPLE

All right. Touché then. But not Mrs Gowan Stevens:
Temple Drake. You remember Temple: the all-
Mississippi debutante whose finishing school was the
Memphis sporting house? About eight years ago, remember? Not that anyone, certainly not the sovereign state of Mississippi's first paid servant, need be
reminded of that, provided they could read newspapers eight years ago or were kin to somebody who
could read eight years ago or even had a friend who
could or even just hear or even just remember or just
believe the worst or even just hope for it.

GOVERNOR

I think I remember. What has Temple Drake to tell me
then?

TEMPLE

> That's not first. The first thing is, how much will I have
> to tell? I mean, how much of it that you dont already
> know, so that I wont be wasting all of our times telling
> it over? It's two oclock in the morning; you want to—
> maybe even need to—sleep some, even if you are our
> first paid servant; maybe even because of that—— You
> see? I'm already lying. What does it matter to me how
> much sleep the state's first paid servant loses, anymore
> than it matters to the first paid servant, a part of whose
> job is being paid to lose sleep over Nancy Mannigoes
> and Temple Drakes?

STEVENS

> Not lying.

TEMPLE

> All right. Stalling, then. So maybe if his excellency or
> his honor or whatever they call him, will answer the
> question, we can get on.

STEVENS

> Why not let the question go, and just get on?

GOVERNOR (*to Temple*)

> Ask me your question. How much of what do I already
> know?

TEMPLE (*after a moment: she doesn't answer at first, star-
> ing at the Governor: then:*)

> Uncle Gavin's right. Maybe you are the one to ask the
> questions. Only, make it as painless as possible. Be-
> cause it's going to be a little . . . . painful, to put it eu-
> phoniously—at least 'euphonious' is right, isn't it?—no
> matter who bragged about blindfolds.

GOVERNOR

Tell me about Nancy—Mannihoe, Mannikoe—how does she spell it?

TEMPLE

She doesn't. She cant. She cant read or write either. You are hanging her under Mannigoe, which may be wrong too, though after tomorrow morning it wont matter.

GOVERNOR

Oh yes, Manigault. The old Charleston name.

STEVENS

Older than that. Maingault. Nancy's heritage—or anyway her patronym—runs Norman blood.

GOVERNOR

Why not start by telling me about her.

TEMPLE

You are so wise. She was a dope-fiend whore that my husband and I took out of the gutter to nurse our children. She murdered one of them and is to be hung tomorrow morning. We—her lawyer and I—have come to ask you to save her.

GOVERNOR

Yes. I know all that. Why?

TEMPLE

Why am I, the mother whose child she murdered, asking you to save her? Because I have forgiven her.

> (*the Governor watches her, he and Stevens both
> do, waiting. She stares back at the Governor,
> steadily, not defiant: just alert*)

Because she was crazy.

> (*the Governor watches her: she stares back,
> puffing rapidly at the cigarette*)

All right. You dont mean why I am asking you to save
her, but why I—we hired a whore and a tramp and a
dope-fiend to nurse our children.

> (*she puffs rapidly, talking through the smoke*)

To give her another chance—a human being too, even
a nigger dope-fiend whore——

STEVENS

Nor that, either.

TEMPLE (*rapidly, with a sort of despair*)

Oh yes, not even stalling now. Why cant you stop
lying? You know: just stop for a while or a time like
you can stop playing tennis or running or dancing or
drinking or eating sweets during Lent. You know:
not to reform: just to quit for a while, clear your sys-
tem, rest up for a new tune or set or lie? All right. It
was to have someone to talk to. And now you see? I'll
have to tell the rest of it in order to tell you why I
had to have a dope-fiend whore to talk to, why Temple Drake, the white woman, the all-Mississippi
debutante, descendant of long lines of statesmen and
soldiers high and proud in the high proud annals of
our sovereign state, couldn't find anybody except a
nigger dope-fiend whore that could speak her language——

GOVERNOR

Yes. This far, this late at night. Tell it.

TEMPLE (*she puffs rapidly at the cigarette, leans and crushes it out in the ashtray and sits erect again. She speaks in a hard rapid brittle emotionless voice*) Whore, dope-fiend; hopeless, already damned before she was ever born, whose only reason for living was to get the chance to die a murdress on the gallows.—Who not only entered the home of the socialite Gowan Stevenses out of the gutter, but made her debut into the public life of her native city while lying in the gutter with a white man trying to kick her teeth or at least her voice back down her throat.—You remember, Gavin: what was his name? it was before my time in Jefferson, but you remember: the cashier in the bank, the pillar of the church or anyway in the name of his childless wife; and this Monday morning and still drunk, Nancy comes up while he is unlocking the front door of the bank and fifty people standing at his back to get in, and Nancy comes into the crowd and right up to him and says, 'Where's my two dollars, white man?' and he turned and struck her, knocked her across the pavement into the gutter and then ran after her, stomping and kicking at her face or anyway her voice which was still saying 'Where's my two dollars, white man?' until the crowd caught and held him still kicking at the face lying in the gutter, spitting blood and teeth and still saying, 'It was two dollars more than two weeks ago and you done been back twice since' ——

She stops speaking, presses both hands to her face for an instant, then removes them.

TEMPLE

No, no handkerchief; Lawyer Stevens and I made a dry
run on handkerchiefs before we left home tonight.
Where was I?

GOVERNOR (*quotes her*)

'It was already two dollars' ——

TEMPLE

So now I've got to tell all of it. Because that was just
Nancy Mannigoe. Temple Drake was in more than
just a two-dollar Saturday night house. But then, I said
touché, didn't I?

She leans forward and starts to take up the crushed cigarette
from the ashtray. Stevens picks up the pack from the desk and
prepares to offer it to her. She withdraws her hand from the
crushed cigarette and sits back.

TEMPLE (*to the proffered cigarette in Stevens' hand*)

No thanks; I wont need it, after all. From here out, it's
merely anticlimax. *Coup de grace.* The victim never
feels that, does he?—Where was I?

(*quickly*)

Never mind. I said that before too, didn't I?

(*she sits for a moment, her hands gripped in her
lap, motionless*)

There seems to be some of this, quite a lot of this,
which even our first paid servant is not up on; maybe
because he has been our first paid servant for less than
two years yet. Though that's wrong too; he could read
eight years ago, couldn't he? In fact, he couldn't have
been elected governor of even Mississippi if he hadn't

been able to read at least three years in advance, could
he?

STEVENS
Temple.

TEMPLE (*to Stevens*)
Why not? It's just stalling, isn't it?

GOVERNOR (*watching Temple*)
Hush, Gavin.
(*to Temple*)
Coup de grace not only means mercy, but is. Deliver it.
Give her the cigarette, Gavin.

TEMPLE (*sits forward again*)
No thanks. Really.
(*after a second*)
Sorry.
(*quickly*)
You'll notice, I always remember to say that, always remember my manners,—'raising' as we put it. Showing
that I really sprang from gentlefolks, not Norman
knights like Nancy did, but at least people who dont
insult the host in his own house, especially at two
oclock in the morning. Only, I just sprang too far,
where Nancy merely stumbled modestly: a lady again,
you see.
(*after a moment*)
There again. I'm not even lying now: I'm faulting—
what do they call it? burking. You know: here we are
at the fence again; we've got to jump it this time, or
crash. You know: slack the snaffle, let her mouth it a
little, take hold, a light hold, just enough to have

something to jump against; then touch her. So here we are, right back where we started, and so we can start over. So how much will I have to tell, say, speak out loud so that anybody with ears can hear it, about Temple Drake that I never thought that anything on earth, least of all the murder of my child and the execution of a nigger dope-fiend whore, would ever make me tell? That I came here at two oclock in the morning to wake you up to listen to, after eight years of being safe or at least quiet? You know: how much will I have to tell, to make it good and painful of course, but quick too, so that you can revoke or commute the sentence or whatever you do to it, and we can all go back home to sleep or at least to bed? Painful of course, but just painful enough —— I think you said 'euphoniously' was right, didn't you?

GOVERNOR

Death is painful. A shameful one, even more so— which is not too euphonious, even at best.

TEMPLE

Oh, death. We're not talking about death now. We're talking about shame. Nancy Mannigoe has no shame; all she has is, to die. But touché for me too; haven't I brought Temple Drake all the way here at two oclock in the morning for the reason that all Nancy Mannigoe has, is to die?

STEVENS

Tell him, then.

TEMPLE

He hasn't answered my question yet.

(*to Governor*)

Try to answer it. How much will I have to tell? Dont just say 'everything'. I've already heard that.

GOVERNOR

I know who Temple Drake was: the young woman student at the University eight years ago who left the school one morning on a special train of students to attend a baseball game at another college, and disappeared from the train somewhere during its run, and vanished, nobody knew where, until she reappeared six weeks later as a witness in a murder trial in Jefferson, produced by the lawyer of the man who, it was then learned, had abducted her and held her prisoner——

TEMPLE

—in the Memphis sporting house: dont forget that.

GOVERNOR

—in order to produce her to prove his alibi in the murder——

TEMPLE

—that Temple Drake knew had done the murder for the very good reason that——

STEVENS

Wait. Let me play too. She got off the train at the instigation of a young man who met the train at an intermediate stop with an automobile, the plan being to drive on to the ball game in the car, except that the young man was drunk at the time and got drunker, and wrecked the car and stranded both of them at the moonshiner's house where the murder happened, and from which the murderer kidnapped her and carried her to Memphis, to hold her until he would need his alibi. Afterward he—the young man with the automobile, her escort and protector at the moment of the abduction—married her. He is her husband now. He is my nephew.

TEMPLE (*to Stevens, bitterly*)

You too. So wise too. Why cant you believe in truth? At least that I'm trying to tell it. At least trying now to tell it.

(*to Governor*)

Where was I?

GOVERNOR (*quotes*)

That Temple Drake knew had done the murder for the very good reason that——

TEMPLE

Oh yes. —for the very good reason that she saw him do it, or at least his shadow: and so produced by his lawyer in the Jefferson courtroom so that she could swear away the life of the man who was accused of it. Oh yes, that's the one. And now I've already told you something you nor nobody else but the Memphis lawyer knew, and I haven't even started. You see? I cant even bargain with you. You haven't even said yes or no yet, whether you can save her or not, whether you want to save her or not, will consider saving her or not; which, if either of us, Temple Drake or Mrs Gowan Stevens either, had any sense, would have demanded first of you.

GOVERNOR

Do you want to ask me that first?

TEMPLE

I cant. I dont dare. You might say no.

GOVERNOR

Then you wouldn't have to tell me about Temple Drake.

TEMPLE

I've got to do that. I've got to say it all, or I wouldn't be here. But unless I can still believe that you might say yes, I dont see how I can. Which is another touché for somebody: God, maybe—if there is one. You see? That's what's so terrible. We dont even need Him. Simple evil is enough. Even after eight years, it's still enough. It was eight years ago that Uncle Gavin said— oh yes, he was there too; didn't you just hear him? He could have told you all of this or anyway most of it over the telephone and you could be in bed asleep right this minute—said how there is a corruption even in just looking at evil, even by accident; that you cant haggle, traffic, with putrefaction—you cant, you dont dare——

(*she stops, tense, motionless*)

GOVERNOR

Take the cigarette now.

(*to Stevens*)

Gavin——

(*Stevens takes up the pack and prepares to offer the cigarette*)

TEMPLE

No thanks. It's too late now. Because here we go. If we cant jump the fence, we can at least break through it——

STEVENS (*interrupts*)

Which means that anyway one of us will get over standing up.

(*as Temple reacts*)

Oh yes, I'm still playing; I'm going to ride this one too. Go ahead.

(*prompting*)

Temple Drake——

TEMPLE

—Temple Drake, the foolish virgin; that is, a virgin as far as anybody went on record to disprove, but a fool certainly by anybody's standards and computation; seventeen, and more of a fool than simply being a virgin or even being seventeen could excuse or account for; indeed, showing herself capable of a height of folly which even seven or three, let alone mere virginity, could scarcely have matched——

STEVENS

Give the brute a chance. Try at least to ride him at the fence and not just through it.

TEMPLE

You mean the Virginia gentleman.

(*to Governor*)

That's my husband. He went to the University of Virginia, trained, Uncle Gavin would say, at Virginia not only in drinking but in gentility too——

STEVENS

—and ran out of both at the same instant that day
eight years ago when he took her off the train and
wrecked the car at the moonshiner's house.

TEMPLE

But relapsed into one of them at least because at least
he married me as soon as he could.
(*to Stevens*)
You dont mind my telling his excellency that, do you?

STEVENS

A relapse into both of them. He hasn't had a drink
since that day either. His excellency might bear that in
mind too.

GOVERNOR

I will. I have.
(*he makes just enough of a pause to cause them*
both to stop and look at him)
I almost wish ——
(*they are both watching him; this is the first in-*
timation we have that something is going on
here, an undercurrent: that the Governor and
Stevens know something which Temple doesn't:
to Temple)
He didn't come with you.

STEVENS (*mildly yet quickly*)
Wont there be time for that later, Henry?

TEMPLE (*quick, defiant, suspicious, hard*)
Who didn't?

GOVERNOR
    Your husband.

TEMPLE (*quick and hard*)
    Why?

GOVERNOR
    You have come here to plead for the life of the mur-
    dress of your child. Your husband was its parent too.

TEMPLE
    You're wrong. We didn't come here at two oclock in the
    morning to save Nancy Mannigoe. Nancy Mannigoe is
    not even concerned in this because Nancy Mannigoe's
    lawyer told me before we ever left Jefferson that you were
    not going to save Nancy Mannigoe. What we came here
    and waked you up at two oclock in the morning for is just
    to give Temple Drake a good fair honest chance to suf-
    fer—you know: just anguish for the sake of anguish, like
    that Russian or somebody who wrote a whole book about
    suffering, not suffering for or about anything, just suffer-
    ing, like somebody unconscious not really breathing for
    anything but just breathing. Or maybe that's wrong too
    and nobody really cares, suffers, anymore about suffering
    than they do about truth or justice or Temple Drake's
    shame or Nancy Mannigoe's worthless nigger life ——

    She stops speaking, sitting quite still, erect in the chair,
    her face raised slightly, not looking at either of them
    while they watch her.

GOVERNOR
    Give her the handkerchief now.

Stevens takes a fresh handkerchief from his pocket, shakes it
out and extends it toward Temple. She does not move, her
hands still clasped in her lap. Stevens rises, crosses, drops the
handkerchief into her lap, returns to his chair.

TEMPLE

Thanks really. But it doesn't matter now; we're too near
the end; you could almost go on down to the car and
start it and have the engine warming up while I finish.
(*to Governor*)
You see? All you'll have to do now is just be still and listen. Or not even listen if you dont want to: but just be
still, just wait. And not long either now, and then we
can all go to bed and turn off the light. And then,
night: dark: sleep even maybe, when with the same
arm you turn off the light and pull the covers up with,
you can put away forever Temple Drake and whatever
it is you have done about her, and Nancy Mannigoe
and whatever it is you have done about her, if you're
going to do anything, if it even matters anyhow
whether you do anything or not, and none of it will
ever have to bother us anymore. Because Uncle Gavin
was only partly right. It's not that you must never even
look on evil and corruption; sometimes you cant help
that, you are not always warned. It's not even that you
must resist it always. Because you've got to start much
sooner than that. You've got to be already prepared to
resist it, say no to it, long before you see it; you must
have already said no to it long before you even know
what it is. I'll have the cigarette now, please.

Stevens takes up the pack, rising and working the end
of a cigarette free, and extends the pack. She takes the

cigarette, already speaking again while Stevens puts the pack on the desk and takes up the lighter which the Governor, watching Temple, shoves across the desk where Stevens can reach it. Stevens snaps the lighter on and holds it out. Temple makes no effort to light the cigarette, holding the cigarette in her hand and talking. Then she lays the cigarette unlighted on the ashtray and Stevens closes the lighter and sits down again, putting the lighter down beside the pack of cigarettes.

TEMPLE

Because Temple Drake liked evil. She only went to the ball game because she would have to get on a train to do it, so that she could slip off the train the first time it stopped, and get into the car to drive a hundred miles with a man——

STEVENS

—who couldn't hold his drink.

TEMPLE (*to Stevens*)

All right. Aren't I just saying that?
(*to Governor*)
An optimist. Not the young man; he was just doing the best he knew, could. It wasn't him that suggested the trip: it was Temple——

STEVENS

It was his car though. Or his mother's.

TEMPLE (*to Stevens*)

All right. All right.
(*to Governor*)

No, Temple was the optimist: not that she had foreseen, planned ahead either: she just had unbounded
faith that her father and brothers would know evil
when they saw it, so all she had to do was, do the one
thing which she knew they would forbid her to do if
they had the chance. And they were right about the
evil, and so of course she was right too, though even
then it was not easy: she even had to drive the car for a
while after we began to realise that the young man was
wrong, had graduated too soon in the drinking part of
his Virginia training——

STEVENS
It was Gowan who knew the moonshiner and insisted
on going there.

TEMPLE
—and even then——

STEVENS
He was driving when you wrecked.

TEMPLE (*to Stevens: quick and harsh*)
And married me for it. Does he have to pay for it
twice? It wasn't really worth paying for once, was it?
(*to Governor*)
And even then——

GOVERNOR
How much was it worth?

TEMPLE
Was what worth?

GOVERNOR

His marrying you.

TEMPLE

You mean to him, of course. Less than he paid for it.

GOVERNOR

Is that what he thinks too?
    (*they stare at one another, Temple alert, quite
    watchful, though rather impatient than any-
    thing else*)
You're going to tell me something that he doesn't know,
else you would have brought him with you. Is that right?

TEMPLE

Yes.

GOVERNOR

Would you tell it if he were here?
    (*Temple is staring at the Governor. Unnoticed
    by her, Stevens makes a faint movement. The
    Governor stops him with a slight motion of one
    hand which also Temple does not notice*)
Now that you have come this far, now that, as you said,
you have got to tell it, say it aloud, not to save Nan—
this woman, but because you decided before you left
home tonight that there is nothing else to do but tell it.

TEMPLE

How do I know whether I would or not?

GOVERNOR

Suppose he was here—sitting in that chair where
Gav—your uncle is——

TEMPLE

—or behind the door or in one of your desk drawers,
maybe? He's not. He's at home. I gave him a sleeping
pill.

GOVERNOR

But suppose he was, now that you have got to say it.
Would you still say it?

TEMPLE

All right. Yes. Now will you please shut up too and let
me tell it? How can I, if you and Gavin wont hush and
let me? I cant even remember where I was.—Oh yes.
So I saw the murder, or anyway the shadow of it, and
the man took me to Memphis, and I know that too, I
had two legs and I could see, and I could have simply
screamed up the main street of any of the little towns
we passed, just as I could have walked away from the
car after Gow—we ran it into the tree, and stopped a
wagon or a car which would have carried me to the
nearest town or railroad station or even back to school
or for that matter, right on back home into my father's
or brothers' hands. But not me, not Temple. I choose
the murderer——

STEVENS (*to Governor*)

He was a psychopath, though that didn't come out in
the trial, and when it did come out, or could have
come out, it was too late. I was there; I saw that too: a
little black thing with an Italian name, like a neat and
only slightly deformed cockroach: a hybrid, sexually
incapable. But then, she will tell you that too.

TEMPLE (*with bitter sarcasm*)

Dear Uncle Gavin.

> (*to Governor*)

Oh yes, that too, her bad luck too: to plump for a thing which didn't even have sex for his weakness, but just murder——

> (*she stops, sitting motionless, erect, her hands clenched on her lap, her eyes closed*)

If you both would just hush, just let me. I seem to be like trying to drive a hen into a barrel. Maybe if you would just try to act like you wanted to keep her out of it, from going into it——

GOVERNOR

Dont call it a barrel. Call it a tunnel. That's a thoroughfare, because the other end is open too. Go through it. There was no—sex.

TEMPLE

Not from him. He was worse than a father or uncle. It was worse than being the wealthy ward of the most indulgent trust or insurance company: carried to Memphis and shut up in that Manuel Street sporting house like a ten-year-old bride in a Spanish convent, with the madam herself more eagle-eyed than any mamma— and the Negro maid to guard the door while the madam would be out, to wherever she would go, wherever the madams of cat houses go on their afternoons out, to pay police court fines or protection or to the bank or maybe just visiting, which would not be so bad because the maid would unlock the door and come inside and we could——

> (*she falters, pauses for less than a second; then quickly*)

Yes, that's why—talk. A prisoner of course, and maybe not in a very gilded cage, but at least the prisoner was. I had perfume by the quart; some salesgirl chose it of course, and it was the wrong kind, but at least I had it, and he bought me a fur coat—with nowhere to wear it of course because he wouldn't let me out, but I had the coat—and snazzy underwear and negligees, selected also by salesgirls but at least the best or anyway the most expensive—the taste at least of the big end of an underworld big shot's wallet. Because he wanted me to be contented, you see; and not only contented, he didn't even mind if I was happy too: just so I was there when or in case the police finally connected him with that Mississippi murder; not only didn't mind if I was happy, he even made the effort himself to see that I was. And so at last we have come to it, because now I have got to tell you this too to give you a valid reason why I waked you up at two in the morning to ask you to save a murdress.

She stops speaking, reaches and takes the unlighted cigarette from the tray, then realises it is unlit. Stevens takes up the lighter from the desk and starts to get up. Still watching Temple, the Governor makes to Stevens a slight arresting signal with his hand. Stevens pauses, then pushes the lighter along the desk to where Temple can reach it, and sits back down. Temple takes the lighter, snaps it on, lights the cigarette, closes the lighter and puts it back on the desk. But after only one puff at the cigarette, she lays it back on the tray and sits again as before, speaking again.

TEMPLE
    Because I still had the two arms and legs and eyes; I could have climbed down the rainspout at any time,

the only difference being that I didn't. I would never leave the room except late at night, when he would come in a closed car the size of an undertaker's wagon, and he and the chauffeur on the front seat, and me and the madam in the back, rushing at forty and fifty and sixty miles an hour up and down the back alleys of the redlight district. Which—the back alleys—was all I ever saw of them too. I was not even permitted to meet or visit with or even see the other girls in my own house, not even to sit with them after work and listen to the shop talk while they counted their chips or blisters or whatever they would do sitting on one another's beds in the elected dormitory. . . .

   (*she pauses again, continues in a sort of surprise, amazement*)

Yes, it was like the dormitory at school: the smell: of women, young women all busy thinking not about men but just man: only a little stronger, a little calmer, less excited,—sitting on the temporarily idle beds discussing the exigencies—that's surely the right one, isn't it?—of their trade. But not me, not Temple: shut up in that room twenty-four hours a day, with nothing to do but hold fashion shows in the fur coat and the flash pants and negligees, with nothing to see it but a two-foot mirror and a Negro maid; hanging bone dry and safe in the middle of sin and pleasure like being suspended twenty fathoms deep in an ocean diving bell. Because he wanted her to be contented, you see. He even made the last effort himself. But Temple didn't want to be just contented. So she had to do what us sporting girls call fall in love.

GOVERNOR
   Ah.

STEVENS
   That's right.

TEMPLE (*quickly: to Stevens*)
   Hush.

STEVENS (*to Temple*)
   Hush yourself.
       (*to Governor*)
   He—Vitelli—they called him Popeye—brought the
   man there himself. He—the young man——

TEMPLE
   Gavin! No, I tell you!

STEVENS (*to Temple*)
   You are drowning in an orgasm of abjectness and moderation when all you need is truth.
       (*to Governor*)
   —was known in his own circles as Red, Alabama Red;
   not to the police, or not officially, since he was not a
   criminal, or anyway not yet, but just a thug, probably
   cursed more by simple eupepsia than by anything else.
   He was a houseman—the bouncer—at the nightclub,
   joint, on the outskirts of town, which Popeye owned
   and which was Popeye's headquarters. He died shortly
   afterward in the alley behind Temple's prison, of a bul-
   let from the same pistol which had done the Mississippi murder, though Popeye too was dead, hanged in
   Alabama for a murder he did not commit, before the
   pistol was ever found and connected with him.

GOVERNOR

I see. This—Popeye——

STEVENS

—discovered himself betrayed by one of his own servants, and took a princely vengeance on his honor's
smircher? You will be wrong. You underrate this *pre-
cieux*, this flower, this jewel. Vitelli. What a name for
him. A hybrid, impotent. He was hanged the next year,
to be sure. But even that was wrong: his very efface-
ment debasing, flouting, even what dignity man has
been able to lend to necessary human abolishment.
He should have been crushed somehow under a vast
and mindless boot, like a spider. He didn't sell her; you
violate and outrage his very memory with that crass
and material impugnment. He was a purist, an amateur always; he did not even murder for base profit. It
was not even for simple lust. He was a gourmet, a
sybarite, centuries, perhaps hemispheres before his
time; in spirit and glands he was of that age of princely
despots to whom the ability even to read was vulgar
and plebeian and, reclining on silk amid silken airs
and scents, had eunuch slaves for that office, commanding death to the slave at the end of each reading,
each evening, that none else alive, even a eunuch
slave, shall have shared in, partaken of, remembered,
the poem's evocation.

GOVERNOR

I dont think I understand.

STEVENS

Try to. Uncheck your capacity for rage and revulsion—the sort of rage and revulsion it takes to step on

a worm. If Vitelli cannot evoke that in you, his life will have been indeed a desert.

TEMPLE

Or dont try to. Just let it go. Just for God's sake let it go. I met the man, how doesn't matter, and I fell what I called in love with him and what it was or what I called it doesn't matter either because all that matters is that I wrote the letters ——

GOVERNOR

I see. This is the part that her husband didn't know.

TEMPLE (*to Governor*)

And what does that matter either? Whether he knows or not? What can another face or two or name or two matter, since he knows that I lived for six weeks in a Manuel Street brothel? Or another body or two in the bed? Or three or four? I'm trying to tell it, enough of it. Cant you see that? But cant you make him let me alone so I can. Make him, for God's sake, let me alone.

GOVERNOR (*to Stevens: watching Temple*)

No more, Gavin.
      (*to Temple*)
So you fell in love.

TEMPLE

Thank you for that. I mean, the 'love.' Except that I didn't even fall, I was already there: the bad, the lost: who could have climbed down the gutter or lightning rod any time and got away, or even simpler than that:

disguised myself as the nigger maid with a stack of towels and a bottle opener and change for ten dollars, and walked right out the front door. So I wrote the letters. I would write one each time . . . afterward, after they— he left, and sometimes I would write two or three when it would be two or three days between, when they—he wouldn't——

GOVERNOR

What? What's that?

TEMPLE

—you know: something to do, be doing, filling the time, better than the fashion parades in front of the two-foot glass with nobody to be disturbed even by the . . . pants, or even no pants. Good letters——

GOVERNOR

Wait. What did you say?

TEMPLE

I said they were good letters, even for——

GOVERNOR

You said, after *they* left.

> (*they look at one another. Temple doesn't answer: to Stevens, though still watching Temple*)

Am I being told that this . . . Vitelli would be there in the room too?

STEVENS

Yes. That was why he brought him. You can see now what I meant by connoisseur and gourmet.

GOVERNOR

And what you meant by the boot too. But he's dead.
You know that.

STEVENS

Oh yes. He's dead. And I said 'purist' too. To the last:
hanged the next summer in Alabama for a murder he
didn't even commit and which nobody involved in the
matter really believed he had committed, only not
even his lawyer could persuade him to admit that he
couldn't have done it if he had wanted to, or wouldn't
have done it if the notion had struck him. Oh yes, he's
dead too; we haven't come here for vengeance.

GOVERNOR (*to Temple*)

Yes. Go on. The letters.

TEMPLE

The letters. They were good letters. I mean —— good
ones.
   (*staring steadily at the Governor*)
What I'm trying to say is, they were the kind of letters
that if you had written them to a man, even eight years
ago, you wouldn't—would—rather your husband didn't
see them, no matter what he thought about your—
past.
   (*still staring at the Governor as she makes her
   painful confession*)
Better than you would expect from a seventeen-year-
old amateur. I mean, you would have wondered how
anybody just seventeen and not even through fresh-
man in college, could have learned the—right words.
Though all you would have needed probably would be

an old dictionary from back in Shakespeare's time when, so they say, people hadn't learned how to blush at words. That is, anybody except Temple Drake, who didn't need a dictionary, who was a fast learner and so even just one lesson would have been enough for her, let alone three or four or a dozen or two or three dozen.

(*staring at the Governor*)

No, not even one lesson because the bad was already there waiting, who hadn't even heard yet that you must be already resisting the corruption not only before you look at it but before you even know what it is, what you are resisting. So I wrote the letters, I dont know how many, enough, more than enough because just one would have been enough. And that's all.

GOVERNOR

All?

TEMPLE

Yes. You've certainly heard of blackmail. The letters turned up again of course. And of course, being Temple Drake, the first way to buy them back that Temple Drake thought of, was to produce the material for another set of them.

STEVENS (*to Temple*)

Yes, that's all. But you've got to tell him why it's all.

TEMPLE

I thought I had. I wrote some letters that you would have thought that even Temple Drake might have been ashamed to put on paper, and then the man I

wrote them to died, and I married another man and reformed, or thought I had, and bore two children and
hired another reformed whore so that I would have
somebody to talk to, and I even thought I had forgotten about the letters until they turned up again and
then I found out that I not only hadn't forgot about the
letters, I hadn't even reformed——

STEVENS

All right. Do you want me to tell it, then?

TEMPLE

And you were the one preaching moderation.

STEVENS

I was preaching against orgasms of it.

TEMPLE (*bitterly*)

Oh, I know. Just suffering. Not for anything: just suffering. Just because it's good for you, like calomel or
ipecac.
    (*to Governor*)
All right. What?

GOVERNOR

The young man died——

TEMPLE

Oh yes.—Died, shot from a car while he was slipping up
the alley behind the house, to climb up the same drain-
pipe I could have climbed down at any time and got
away, to see me—the one time, the first time, the only
time when we thought we had dodged, fooled him,

could be alone together, just the two of us, after all the . . . other ones.—If love can be, mean anything, except the newness, the learning, the peace, the privacy: no shame: not even conscious that you are naked because you are just using the nakedness because that's a part of it; then he was dead, killed, shot down right in the middle of thinking about me, when in just one more minute maybe he would have been in the room with me, when all of him except just his body was already in the room with me and the door locked at last for just the two of us alone, and then it was all over and as though it had never been, happened, it had to be as though it had never happened, except that that was even worse ——

(*rapidly*)

Then the courtroom in Jefferson and I didn't care, not about anything anymore, and my father and brothers waiting and then the year in Europe, Paris, and I still didn't care, and then after a while it really did get easier. You know. People are lucky. They are wonderful. At first you think that you can bear only so much and then you will be free. Then you find out that you can bear anything, you really can and then it wont even matter. Because suddenly it could be as if it had never been, never happened. You know: somebody— Hemingway, wasn't it?—wrote a book about how it had never actually happened to a g—woman, if she just refused to accept it, no matter who remembered, bragged. And besides, the ones who could—remember were both dead. Then Gowan came to Paris that winter and we were married—at the Embassy, with a reception afterward at the Crillon, and if that couldn't fumigate an American past, what else this side of heaven could you hope for to remove stink? Not to mention a new automobile and a honeymoon in a rented hideaway built for his European mistress by a Mohammedan prince at Cap Ferrat. Only——

(*she pauses, falters, for just an instant, then goes on*)

—we—I thought we—I didn't want to efface the stink really——

(*rapidly now, tense, erect, her hands gripped again into fists on her lap*)

You know: just the marriage would be enough: not the Embassy and the Crillon and Cap Ferrat but just to kneel down, the two of us, and say 'We have sinned, forgive us'. And then maybe there would be the love this time—the peace, the quiet, the no shame that I . . . . didn't——missed that other time——

(*falters again, then rapidly again, glib and succinct*)

Love, but more than love too: not depending on just love to hold two people together, make them better than either one would have been alone, but tragedy, suffering, having suffered and caused grief; having something to have to live with even when, because, you knew both of you could never forget it. And then I began to believe something even more than that: that there was something even better, stronger, than tragedy to hold two people together: forgiveness. Only, that seemed to be wrong. Only maybe it wasn't the forgiveness that was wrong, but the gratitude; and maybe the only thing worse than having to give gratitude constantly all the time, is having to accept it——

STEVENS

Which is exactly backward. What was wrong wasn't——

GOVERNOR

Gavin.

STEVENS

Shut up yourself, Henry. What was wrong wasn't Temple's good name. It wasn't even her husband's conscience. It was his vanity: the Virginia-trained aristocrat caught with his gentility around his knees like the guest in the trick Hollywood bathroom. So the forgiving wasn't enough for him, or perhaps he hadn't read Hemingway's book. Because after about a year, his restiveness under the onus of accepting the gratitude began to take the form of doubting the paternity of their child.

TEMPLE

Oh God. Oh God.

GOVERNOR

Gavin.
    (*Stevens stops*)
No more, I said. Call that an order.
    (*to Temple*)
Yes. Tell me.

TEMPLE

I'm trying to. I expected our main obstacle in this would be the bereaved plaintiff. Apparently though it's the defendant's lawyer. I mean, I'm trying to tell you about one Temple Drake, and our Uncle Gavin is showing you another one. So already you've got two different people begging for the same clemency; if everybody concerned keeps on splitting up into two people, you wont even know who to pardon, will you?

And now that I mention it, here we are, already back to
Nancy Mannigoe, and now surely it shouldn't take
long. Let's see, we'd got back to Jefferson too, hadn't
we? Anyway, we are now. I mean, back in Jefferson,
back home. You know: face it: the disgrace: the shame,
face it down, good and down forever, never to haunt us
more; together, a common front to stink because we
love each other and have forgiven all, strong in our
love and mutual forgiveness. Besides having everything else: the Gowan Stevenses, young, popular: a
new bungalow on the right street to start the Saturday
night hangovers in, a country club with a country club
younger set of rallying friends to make it a Saturday
night hangover worthy the name of Saturday night
country club hangover, a pew in the right church to recover from it in provided of course they were not too
hungover even to get to church. Then the son and heir
came; and now we have Nancy: nurse: guide: mentor,
catalyst, glue, whatever you want to call it, holding the
whole lot of them together—not just a magnetic center for the heir apparent and the other little princes or
princesses in their orderly succession, to circle around,
but for the two bigger hunks too of mass or matter or
dirt or whatever it is shaped in the image of God, in a
semblance at least of order and respectability and
peace; not ole cradle-rocking black mammy at all, because the Gowan Stevenses are young and modern, so
young and modern that all the other young country
club set applauded when they took an ex-dope-fiend
nigger whore out of the gutter to nurse their children,
because the rest of the young country club set didn't
know that it wasn't the Gowan Stevenses but Temple
Drake who had chosen the ex-dope-fiend nigger

whore for the reason that an ex-dope-fiend nigger whore was the only animal in Jefferson that spoke Temple Drake's language ——
   (*quickly takes up the burning cigarette from the tray and puffs at it, talking through the puffs*)
Oh yes, I'm going to tell this too. A confidante. You know: the big-time ball player, the idol on the pedestal, the worshipped; and the worshipper, the acolyte, the one that never had and never would, no matter how willing or how hard she tried, get out of the sand-lots, the bush league. You know: the long afternoons, with the last electric button pressed on the last cooking or washing or sweeping gadget and the baby safely asleep for a while, and the two sisters in sin swapping trade or anyway avocational secrets over coca colas in the quiet kitchen. Somebody to talk to, as we all seem to need, want, have to have, not to converse with you nor even agree with you, but just keep quiet and listen. Which is all that people really want, really need; I mean, to behave themselves, keep out of one another's hair; the maladjustments which they tell us breed the arsonists and rapists and murderers and thieves and the rest of the anti-social enemies, are not really maladjustments but simply because the embryonic murderers and thieves didn't have anybody to listen to them: which is an idea the catholic church discovered two thousand years ago only it just didn't carry it far enough or maybe it was too busy being the church to have time to bother with man, or maybe it wasn't the church's fault at all but simply because it had to deal with human beings and maybe if the world was just populated with a kind of creature half of which were dumb, couldn't do anything but listen, couldn't even escape from having to

listen to the other half, there wouldn't even be any war.
Which was what Temple had: somebody paid by the
week just to listen, which you would have thought
would have been enough; and then the other baby
came, the infant, the doomed sacrifice (though of
course we dont know that yet) and you would have
thought that this was surely enough, that now even
Temple Drake would consider herself safe, could be
depended on, having two—what do sailors call them?
oh yes, sheet-anchors—now. Only it wasn't enough.
Because Hemingway was right. I mean, the g—woman
in his book. All you have got to do is, refuse to accept.
Only, you have got to . . . . refuse ——

STEVENS

Now, the letters ——

GOVERNOR (*watching Temple*)

Be quiet, Gavin.

STEVENS

No, I'm going to talk a while now. We'll even stick to
the sports metaphor and call it a relay race, with the senior member of the team carrying the . . . baton, twig,
switch, sapling, tree—whatever you want to call the
symbolical wood, up what remains of the symbolical
hill.

> (*the lights flicker, grow slightly dimmer, then
> flare back up and steady again, as though in a
> signal, a warning*)

The letters. The blackmail. The blackmailer was Red's
younger brother—a criminal of course, but at least a
man ——

TEMPLE

No! No!

STEVENS (*to Temple*)

Be quiet too. It only goes up a hill, not over a precipice. Besides, it's only a stick. The letters were not first. The first thing was the gratitude. And now we have even come to the husband, my nephew. And when I say 'past,' I mean that part of it which the husband knows so far, which apparently was enough in his estimation. Because it was not long before she discovered, realised, that she was going to spend a good part of the rest of her days (nights too) being forgiven for it; in being not only constantly reminded—well, maybe not specifically reminded, but say made—kept— aware of it in order to be forgiven for it so that she might be grateful to the forgiver, but in having to employ more and more of what tact she had—and the patience which she probably didn't know she had, since until now she had never occasion to need patience— to make the gratitude—in which she had probably had as little experience as she had had with patience— acceptable to meet with, match, the high standards of the forgiver. But she was not too concerned. Her husband—my nephew—had made what he probably considered the supreme sacrifice to expiate his part in her past; she had no doubts of her capacity to continue to supply whatever increasing degree of gratitude the increasing appetite—or capacity—of its addict would demand, in return for the sacrifice which, so she believed, she had accepted for the same reason of gratitude. Besides, she still had the legs and the eyes; she could walk away, escape, from it at any moment she

wished, even though her past might have shown her
that she probably would not use the ability to loco-
mote to escape from threat and danger. Do you accept
that?

GOVERNOR

All right. Go on.

STEVENS

Then she discovered that the child—the first one—was
on the way. For that first instant, she must have known
something almost like frenzy. Now she couldn't escape,
she had waited too long. But it was worse than that. It
was as though she realised for the first time that you—
everyone—must, or anyway may have to, pay for your
past; that past is something like a promissory note with a
trick clause in it which, as long as nothing goes wrong,
can be manumitted in an orderly manner, but which
fate or luck or chance, can foreclose on you without
warning. That is, she had known, accepted, this all the
time and dismissed it because she knew that she could
cope, was invulnerable through simple integration,
own-woman-ness. But now there would be a child, tender and defenseless. But you never really give up hope,
you know, not even after you finally realise that people
not only can bear anything, but probably will have to, so
probably even before the frenzy had had time to fade,
she found a hope: which was the child's own tender and
defenseless innocence: that God—if there was one—
would protect the child—not her: she asked no quarter
and wanted none; she could cope, either cope or bear it,
but the child from the sight draft of her past—because it
was innocent, even though she knew better, all her observation having shown her that God either would not

or could not—anyway, did not—save innocence just because it was innocent; that when He said 'Suffer little children to come unto Me' He meant exactly that: He meant suffer; that the adults, the fathers, the old in and capable of sin, must be ready and willing—nay, eager—to suffer at any time, that the little children shall come unto Him unanguished, unterrified, undefiled. Do you accept that?

GOVERNOR

Go on.

STEVENS

So at least she had ease. Not hope: ease. It was precarious of course, a balance, but she could walk a tightrope too. It was as though she had struck, not a bargain, but an armistice with God—if there was one. She had not tried to cheat; she had not tried to evade the promissory note of her past by intervening the blank check of a child's innocence—it was born now, a little boy, a son, her husband's son and heir—between. She had not tried to prevent the child; she had simply never thought about pregnancy in this connection, since it took the physical fact of the pregnancy to reveal to her the existence of that promissory note bearing her post-dated signature. And since God—if there was one—must be aware of that, then she too would bear her side of the bargain by not demanding on Him a second time since He—if there was one—would at least play fair, would be at least a gentleman. And that?

GOVERNOR

Go on.

STEVENS

So you can take your choice about the second child.
Perhaps she was too busy between the three of them
to be careful enough: between the three of them:
the doom, the fate, the past; the bargain with God;
the forgiveness and the gratitude. Like the Juggler
says, not with three insentient replaceable Indian
clubs or balls, but three glass bulbs filled with nitro-
glycerin and not enough hands for one even: one
hand to offer the atonement with and another to receive the forgiveness with and a third needed to offer
the gratitude, and still a fourth hand more and more
imperative as time passed to sprinkle in steadily and
constantly increasing doses a little more and a little
more of the sugar and seasoning on the gratitude to
keep it palatable to its swallower—that perhaps: she
just didn't have time to be careful enough, or perhaps
it was desperation, or perhaps this was when her husband first refuted or implied or anyway impugned—
whichever it was—his son's paternity. Anyway, she
was pregnant again; she had broken her word, destroyed her talisman, and she probably knew fifteen
months before the letters that this was the end, and
when the man appeared with the old letters she probably was not even surprised: she had merely been
wondering for fifteen months what form the doom
would take. And accept this too ——

The lights flicker and dim further, then steady at that point.

STEVENS

And relief too. Because at last it was over; the roof
had fallen, avalanche had roared; even the helpless-

ness and the impotence were finished now, because
now even the old fragility of bone and meat was no
longer a factor;—and, who knows? because of that
fragility, a kind of pride, triumph: you have waited for
destruction: you endured; it was inevitable, inescapable, you had no hope. Nevertheless, you did
not merely cringe, crouching, your head, vision,
buried in your arms; you were not watching that
poised arrestment all the time, true enough, but that
was not because you feared it but because you were
too busy putting one foot before the other, never for
one instant really flagging, faltering, even though you
knew it was in vain;—triumph in the very fragility
which no longer need concern you now, for the reason that the all, the very worst, which catastrophe can
do to you, is crush and obliterate the fragility; you
were the better man, you outfaced even catastrophe,
outlasted it, compelled it to move first; you did not
even defy it, not even contemptuous: with no other
tool or implement but that worthless fragility, you
held disaster off as with one hand you might support
the weightless silken canopy of a bed, for six long
years while it, with all its weight and power, could
not possibly prolong the obliteration of your fragility
over five or six seconds; and even during that five or
six seconds you would still be the better man, since
all that it—the catastrophe—could deprive you of,
you yourself had already written off six years ago as
being, inherently of and because of its own fragile
self, worthless.

GOVERNOR
    And now, the man.

STEVENS

I thought you would see it too. Even the first one stuck
out like a sore thumb. Yes, he ——

GOVERNOR

The first what?

STEVENS (*pauses, looks at the Governor*)

The first man, Red. Dont you know anything at all
about women? I never saw Red or this next one, his
brother, either, but all three of them, the other two and
her husband, probably all look enough alike or act
enough alike—maybe by simply making enough impossible unfulfillable demands on her or by being
drawn to her enough to accept, risk, almost incredible
conditions—to be at least first cousins. Where have
you been all your life?

GOVERNOR

All right. The man.

STEVENS

At first, all he thought of, planned on, was interested
in, intended, was the money—to collect for the letters,
and beat it, get the hell out. Of course, even at the end,
all he was really after was still the money, not only after
he found out that he would have to take her and the
child too to get it, but even when it looked like all he
was going to get, at least for a while, was just a runaway
wife and a six-months-old infant. In fact, Nancy's error,
her really fatal action on that fatal and tragic night, was
in not giving the money and the jewels both to him
when she found where Temple had hidden them, and

getting the letters and getting rid of him forever, instead of hiding the money and jewels from Temple in
her turn—which was what Temple herself thought too
apparently, since she—Temple—told him a lie about
how much the money was, telling him it was only two
hundred dollars when it was actually almost two thousand. So you would have said that he wanted the
money indeed, and just how much, how badly, to have
been willing to pay that price for it. Or maybe he was
being wise—'smart', he would have called it—beyond
his years and time, and without having actually
planned it that way, was really inventing a new and
safe method of kidnapping: that is, pick an adult victim capable of signing her own checks—also with an
infant in arms for added persuasion—and not forcing
but actually persuading her to come along under her
own power and then—still peaceably—extracting the
money later at your leisure, using the tender welfare of
the infant as a fulcrum for your lever. Or maybe we're
both wrong and both should give credit—what little of
it—where credit—what little of it—is due, since it was
just the money with her too at first, though he was
probably still thinking it was just the money at the very
time when, having got her own jewelry together and
found where her husband kept the key to the strongbox (and I imagine, even opened it one night after her
husband was in bed asleep and counted the money in
it or at least made sure there was money in it or anyway
that the key would actually open it), she found herself
still trying to rationalise why she had not paid over the
money and got the letters and destroyed them and so
rid herself forever of her Damocles' roof. Which was
what she did not do. Because Hemingway—his girl—

was quite right: all you have got to do is, refuse to accept it. Only, you have got to be told truthfully beforehand what you must refuse; the gods owe you that—at least a clear picture and a clear choice. Not to be fooled by . . . who knows? probably even gentleness, after a fashion, back there on those afternoons or whenever they were in the Memphis . . . . all right: honeymoon, even with a witness; in this case certainly anything much better lacked, and indeed, who knows? (I am Red now) even a little of awe, incredulous hope, incredulous amazement, even a little of trembling at this much fortune, this much luck dropping out of the very sky itself, into his embrace; at least (Temple now) no gang: even rape become tender: only one, an individual, still refusable, giving her at least (this time) the similitude of being wooed, of an opportunity to say Yes first, letting her even believe she could say either one of yes or no. I imagine that he (the new one, the blackmailer) even looked like his brother—a younger Red, the Red of a few years even before she knew him, and—if you will permit it—less stained, so that in a way it may have seemed to her that here at last even she might slough away the six years' soilure of struggle and repentance and terror to no avail. And if this is what you meant, then you are right too: a man, at least a man, after six years of that sort of forgiving which debased not only the forgiven but the forgiven's gratitude too,—a bad man of course, a criminal by intent regardless of how cramped his opportunities may have been up to this moment; and, capable of blackmail, vicious and not merely competent to, but destined to, bring nothing but evil and disaster and ruin to anyone foolish enough to enter his orbit, cast her lot with his.

But—by comparison, that six years of comparison—at least a man—a man so single, so hard and ruthless, so impeccable in amorality, as to have a kind of integrity, purity, who would not only never need nor intend to forgive anyone anything, he would never even realise that anyone expected him to forgive anyone anything; who wouldn't even bother to forgive her if it ever dawned on him that he had the opportunity, but instead would simply black her eyes and knock a few teeth out and fling her into the gutter: so that she could rest secure forever in the knowledge that, until she found herself with a black eye and or spitting teeth in the gutter, he would never even know he had anything to forgive her for.

This time, the lights do not flicker. They begin to dim steadily toward and then into complete darkness as Stevens continues.

STEVENS

Nancy was the confidante, at first, while she—Nancy—still believed probably that the only problem, factor, was how to raise the money the blackmailer demanded, without letting the boss, the master, the husband find out about it; finding, discovering—this is still Nancy—realising probably that she had not really been a confidante for a good while, a long while before she discovered that what she actually was, was a spy: on her employer: not realising until after she had discovered that, although Temple had taken the money and the jewels too from her husband's strongbox, she—Temple—still hadn't paid them over to the blackmailer and got the letters, that the payment of the money and jewels was less than half of Temple's plan.

The lights go completely out. The stage is in complete darkness. Stevens' voice continues.

STEVENS

That was when Nancy in her turn found where Temple had hidden the money and jewels, and—Nancy—took them in her turn and hid them from Temple; this was the night of the day Gowan left for a week's fishing at Aransas Pass, taking the older child, the boy, with him, to leave the child for a week's visit with its grandparents in New Orleans until Gowan would pick him up on his way home from Texas.

(*to Temple: in the darkness*)

Now. Tell him.

The stage is in complete darkness.

SCENE II

Interior, Temple's private sitting- or dressing-room. 9:30 P.M. September thirteenth *ante.*

The lights go up, lower R, as in Act I in the transition from the courtroom to the Stevens living room, though instead of the living room, the scene is now Temple's private apartment. A door L, enters from the house proper. A door R, leads into the nursery where the child is asleep in its crib. At rear, french windows open onto a terrace; this is a private entrance to the house itself from outdoors. At L, a closet door stands open. Garments are scattered over the floor about it, indicating that the closet has been searched, not hurriedly so much as savagely and ruthlessly and thoroughly. At R, is a fireplace of gas logs. A desk against the rear wall is open and shows traces of the same savage and ruthless search. A table center, bears Temple's hat, gloves and bag, also a bag such as is associated with infants; two bags, obviously Temple's, are packed and closed and sit on the floor beside the table. The whole room indicates Temple's imminent departure, and that something has been vainly yet savagely and completely, perhaps even frantically, searched for.

When the lights go up, Pete is standing in the open closet door, holding a final garment, a negligee, in his hands. He is about 25. He does not look like a criminal. That is, he is not a standardised recognisable criminal or gangster type, quite. He looks almost like the general conception of a college man, or a successful young automobile or appliance salesman. His clothes are ordinary, neither flashy nor sharp, simply what everybody wears. But there is a definite 'untamed' air to him. He is handsome, attractive to women, not at all unpredictable because you—or they—know exactly what he will do, you just hope he wont do it this time. He has a hard, ruthless quality, not immoral but unmoral.

He wears a light weight summer suit, his hat is shoved onto the back of his head so that, engaged as he is at present, he looks exactly like a youthful city detective in a tough moving picture. He is searching the flimsy negligee, quickly and without gentleness, drops it and turns, finds his feet entangled in the other garments on the floor and without pausing, kicks himself free and crosses to the desk and stands looking down at the litter on it which he has already searched thoroughly and savagely once, with a sort of bleak and contemptuous disgust.

Temple enters, L. She wears a dark suit for travelling beneath a light weight open coat, is hatless, carries the fur coat which we have seen, and a child's robe or blanket over the same arm, and a filled milk bottle in the other hand. She pauses long enough to glance at the littered room. Then she comes on in and approaches the table. Pete turns his head; except for that, he doesn't move.

PETE

Well?

TEMPLE

No. The people where she lives say they haven't seen her since she left to come to work this morning.

PETE

I could have told you that.
(*he glances at his wrist watch*)
We've still got time. Where does she live?

TEMPLE (*at the table*)

And then what? hold a lighted cigarette against the sole of her foot?

PETE

It's fifty dollars, even if you are accustomed yourself to thinking in hundreds. Besides the jewelry. What do you suggest then? call the cops?

TEMPLE

No. You wont have to run. I'm giving you an out.

PETE

An out?

TEMPLE

No dough, no snatch. Isn't that how you would say it?

PETE

Maybe I dont get you.

TEMPLE

You can quit now. Clear out. Leave. Get out from under. Save yourself. Then all you'll have to do is, wait till my husband gets back, and start over.

PETE

Maybe I still dont get you.

TEMPLE

You've still got the letters, haven't you?

PETE

Oh, the letters.

He reaches inside his coat, takes out the packet of letters and tosses it onto the table.

There you are.

TEMPLE

I told you two days ago I didn't want them.

PETE

Sure. That was two days ago.

They watch one another a moment. Then Temple dumps the fur coat and the robe from her arm, onto the table, sets the bot-

tle carefully on the table, takes up the packet of letters and extends her other hand to Pete.

TEMPLE
    Give me your lighter.

Pete produces the lighter from his pocket and hands it to her.
That is, he extends it, not moving otherwise, so that she has to
take a step or two toward him to reach and take it. Then she
turns and crosses to the hearth, snaps the lighter on. It misses
fire two or three times, then lights. Pete has not moved, watching her. She stands motionless a moment, the packet of letters
in one hand, the burning lighter in the other. Then she turns
her head and looks back at him. For another moment they
watch one another.

PETE
    Go ahead. Burn them. The other time I gave them to
    you, you turned them down so you could always
    change your mind and back out. Burn them.

They watch one another for another moment. Then she turns
her head and stands now, her face averted, the lighter still
burning. Pete watches her for another moment.

PETE
    Then put that junk down and come here.

She snaps out the lighter, turns, crosses to the table, putting
the packet of letters and the lighter on the table as she passes it,
and goes on to where Pete has not moved. At this moment,
Nancy appears in the door L. Neither of them see her. Pete
puts his arms around Temple.

PETE

>I offered you an out too.
>>(*he draws her closer*)
>Baby.

TEMPLE

>Dont call me that.

PETE (*tightens his arms, caressing and savage too*)

>Red did. I'm as good a man as he was. Aint I?

They kiss. Nancy moves quietly through the door and stops just inside the room, watching them. She now wears the standardised department store maidservant's uniform, but without cap and apron, beneath a light weight open topcoat; on her head is a battered almost shapeless felt hat which must have once belonged to a man. Pete breaks the kiss.

PETE

>Come on. Let's get out of here. I've even got moral or something. I dont even want to put my hands on you in his house ——

He sees Nancy across Temple's shoulder, and reacts. Temple reacts to him, turns quickly and sees Nancy too. Nancy comes on into the room.

TEMPLE (*to Nancy*)

>What are you doing here?

NANCY

>I brought my foot. So he can hold that cigarette against it.

TEMPLE

So you're not just a thief: you're a spy too.

PETE

Maybe she's not a thief either. Maybe she brought it
back.
    (*they watch Nancy, who doesn't answer*)
Or maybe she didn't. Maybe we had better use that
cigarette.
    (*to Nancy*)
How about it? Is that what you came back for, sure
enough?

TEMPLE (*to Pete*)

Hush. Take the bags and go on to the car.

PETE (*to Temple but watching Nancy*)

I'll wait for you. There may be a little something I can
do here, after all.

TEMPLE

Go on, I tell you! Let's for God's sake get away from
here. Go on.

Pete watches Nancy for a moment longer, who stands facing
them but not looking at anything, motionless, almost bemused, her face sad, brooding and inscrutable. Then Pete
turns, goes to the table, picks up the lighter, seems about to
pass on, then pauses again and with almost infinitesimal hesi-
tation, takes up the packet of letters, puts it back inside his
coat, takes up the two packed bags and crosses to the french
window, passing Nancy, who is still looking at nothing and no
one.

PETE (*to Nancy*)

Not that I wouldn't like to, you know. For less than fifty bucks even. For old lang zyne.

He transfers the bags to one hand, opens the french window, starts to exit, pauses half way out and looks back at Temple.

I'll be listening, in case you change your mind about the cigarette.

He goes on out, draws the door to after him. Just before it closes, Nancy speaks.

NANCY

Wait.

Pete stops, begins to open the door again.

TEMPLE (*quickly: to Pete*)

Go on! Go on! For God's sake go on!

Pete exits, shuts the door after him. Nancy and Temple face each other.

NANCY

Maybe I was wrong to think that just hiding that money and diamonds was going to stop you. Maybe I ought to have give it to him yesterday as soon as I found where you had hid it. Then wouldn't nobody between here and Chicago or Texas seen anything of him but his dust.

TEMPLE

So you did steal it. And you saw what good that did,
didn't you?

NANCY

If you can call it stealing, then so can I. Because wasn't
but part of it yours to begin with. Just the diamonds
was yours. Not to mention that money is almost two
thousand dollars, that you told me was just two hundred and that you told him was even less than that, just
fifty. No wonder he wasn't worried—about just fifty
dollars. He wouldn't even be worried if he knowed it
was even the almost two thousand it is, let alone the
two hundred you told me it was. He aint even worried
about whether or not you'll have any money at all
when you get out to the car. He knows that all he's got
to do is, just wait and keep his hand on you and maybe
just mash hard enough with it, and you'll get another
passel of money and diamonds too out of your husband or your pa. Only, this time he'll have his hand on
you and you'll have a little trouble telling him it's just
fifty dollars instead of almost two thousand——

Temple steps quickly forward and slaps Nancy across the face.
Nancy steps back. As she does so, the packet of money and the
jewel box fall to the floor from inside her topcoat. Temple
stops, looking down at the money and jewels. Nancy recovers.

NANCY

Yes, there it is, that caused all the grief and ruin. If you
hadn't been somebody that would have a box of diamonds and a husband that you could find almost two
thousand dollars in his britches pocket while he was
asleep, that man wouldn't have tried to sell you them

letters. Maybe if I hadn't taken and hid it, you would
have give it to him before you come to this. Or maybe if
I had just give it to him yesterday and got the letters, or
maybe if I was to take it out to where he's waiting in that
car right now, and say, Here, man, take your money ——

TEMPLE

Try it. Pick it up and take it out to him, and see. If
you'll wait until I finish packing, you can even carry
the bag.

NANCY

I know. It aint even the letters anymore. Maybe it
never was. It was already there in whoever could write
the kind of letters that even eight years afterward could
still make grief and ruin. The letters never did matter.
You could have got them back at any time; he even
tried to give them to you twice ——

TEMPLE

How much spying have you been doing?

NANCY

All of it.—You wouldn't even needed money and diamonds to get them back. A woman dont need it. All
she needs is womanishness to get anything she wants
from men. You could have done that right here in the
house, without even tricking your husband into going
off fishing.

TEMPLE

A perfect example of whore morality. But then, if I can
say whore, so can you, cant you? Maybe the difference
is, I decline to be one in my husband's house.

NANCY

I aint talking about your husband. I aint even talking
about you. I'm talking about two little children.

TEMPLE

So am I. Why else do you think I sent Bucky on to his
grandmother, except to get him out of a house where
the man he has been taught to call his father, may at
any moment decide to tell him he has none? As
clever a spy as you must surely have heard my husband——

NANCY (*interrupts*)

I've heard him. And I heard you too. You fought
back—that time. Not for yourself, but for that little
child. But now you have quit.

TEMPLE

Quit?

NANCY

Yes. You gave up. You gave up the child too. Willing to
risk never seeing him again maybe.
   (*Temple doesn't answer*)
That's right. You dont need to make no excuses to me.
Just tell me what you must have already strengthened
your mind up to telling all the rest of the folks that are
going to ask you that. You are willing to risk it. Is that
right?
   (*Temple doesn't answer*)
All right. We'll say you have answered it. So that settles
Bucky. Now answer me this one. Who are you going to
leave the other one with?

TEMPLE

Leave her with? A six-months-old baby?

NANCY

That's right. Of course you cant leave her. Not with
nobody. You cant no more leave a six-months-old baby
with nobody while you run away from your husband
with another man, than you can take a six-months-old
baby with you on that trip. That's what I'm talking
about. So maybe you'll just leave it in there in that cradle; it'll cry for a while, but it's too little to cry very loud
and so maybe wont nobody hear it and come med-
dling, especially with the house shut up and locked
until Mr Gowan gets back next week, and probably by
that time it will have hushed ——

TEMPLE

Are you really trying to make me hit you again?

NANCY

Or maybe taking her with you will be just as easy, at
least until the first time you write Mr Gowan or your
pa for money and they dont send it as quick as your
new man thinks they ought to, and he throws you and
the baby both out. Then you can just drop it into a
garbage can and no more trouble to you or anybody,
because then you will be rid of both of them ——
    (*Temple makes a convulsive movement, then
    catches herself*)
Hit me. Light you a cigarette too. I told you and him
both I brought my foot. Here it is.
    (*she raises her foot slightly*)
I've tried everything else; I reckon I can try that too.

TEMPLE (*repressed, furious*)
   Hush. I tell you for the last time. Hush.

NANCY
   I've hushed.

She doesn't move. She is not looking at Temple. There is a
slight change in her voice or manner, though we only realise
later that she is not addressing Temple.

   I've tried. I've tried everything I know. You can see that.

TEMPLE
   Which nobody will dispute. You threatened me with
   my children, and even with my husband—if you can
   call my husband a threat. You even stole my elope-
   ment money. Oh yes, nobody will dispute that you
   tried. Though at least you brought the money back.
   Pick it up.

NANCY
   You said you dont need it.

TEMPLE
   I dont. Pick it up.

NANCY
   No more do I need it.

TEMPLE
   Pick it up, anyway. You can keep your next week's pay
   out of it when you give it back to Mr Gowan.

Nancy stoops and gathers up the money, and gathers the jewelry back into its box, and puts them on the table.

TEMPLE (*quieter*)
    Nancy.
        (*Nancy looks at her*)
    I'm sorry. Why do you force me to this—hitting and
    screaming at you, when you have always been so good
    to my children and me—my husband too—all of us—
    trying to hold us together in a household, a family, that
    anybody should have known all the time couldn't possi-
    bly hold together? even in decency, let alone happiness?

NANCY
    I reckon I'm ignorant. I dont know that yet. Besides, I
    aint talking about any household or happiness
    neither——

TEMPLE (*with sharp command*)
    Nancy!

NANCY
    —I'm talking about two little children——

TEMPLE
    I said, hush.

NANCY
    I cant hush. I'm going to ask you one more time. Are
    you going to do it?

TEMPLE
    Yes!

NANCY
    Maybe I am ignorant. You got to say it out in words
    yourself, so I can hear them. Say, I'm going to do it.

TEMPLE

You heard me. I'm going to do it.

NANCY

Money or no money.

TEMPLE

Money or no money.

NANCY

Children or no children.
     (*Temple doesn't answer*)
To leave one with a man that's willing to believe the
child aint got no father, willing to take the other one to
a man that dont even want no children ——
     (*they stare at one another*)
If you can do it, you can say it.

TEMPLE

Yes! Children or no children! Now get out of here.
Take your part of that money, and get out. Here ——

Temple goes quickly to the table, removes two or three bills
from the mass of banknotes, and hands them to Nancy, who
takes them. Temple takes up the rest of the money, takes up
her bag from the table and opens it. Nancy crosses quietly
toward the nursery, picking up the milk bottle from the table
as she passes, and goes on. With the open bag in one hand
and the money in the other, Temple notices Nancy's movement.

TEMPLE

What are you doing?

NANCY (*still moving*)
   This bottle has got cold. I'm going to warm it in the
   bathroom.

Then Nancy stops and looks back at Temple, with something
so strange in her look that Temple, about to resume putting the
money into the bag, pauses too, watching Nancy. When
Nancy speaks, it is like the former speech: we dont realise until
afterward what it signifies.

NANCY
   I tried everything I knowed. You can see that.

TEMPLE (*peremptory, commanding*)
   Nancy.

NANCY (*quietly, turning on*)
   I've hushed.

She exits through the door into the nursery. Temple finishes
putting the money into the bag, and closes it and puts it back
on the table. Then she turns to the baby's bag. She tidies it,
checks rapidly over its contents, takes up the jewel box and
stows it in the bag and closes the bag. All this takes about two
minutes; she has just closed the bag when Nancy emerges quietly from the nursery, without the milk bottle, and crosses,
pausing at the table only long enough to put back on it the
money Temple gave her, then starts on toward the opposite
door through which she first entered the room.

TEMPLE
   Now what?

Nancy goes on toward the other door. Temple watches her.

> Nancy.
>> (*Nancy pauses, still not looking back*)
>
> Dont think too hard of me.
>> (*Nancy waits, immobile, looking at nothing. When Temple doesn't continue, she moves again toward the door*)
>
> If I—it ever comes up, I'll tell everybody you did your best. You tried. But you were right. It wasn't even the letters. It was me.
>> (*Nancy moves on*)
>
> Goodbye, Nancy.
>> (*Nancy reaches the door*)
>
> You've got your key. I'll leave your money here on the table. You can get it——
>> (*Nancy exits*)
>
> Nancy!

There is no answer. Temple looks a moment longer at the empty door, shrugs, moves, takes up the money Nancy left, glances about, crosses to the littered desk and takes up a paperweight and returns to the table and puts the money beneath the weight; now moving rapidly and with determination, she takes up the blanket from the table and crosses to the nursery door and exits through it. A second or two, then she screams. The lights flicker and begin to dim, fade swiftly into complete darkness, over the scream.

The stage is in complete darkness.

SCENE III

Same as Scene I. Governor's Office. 3:09 A.M. March twelfth.

The lights go on upper L. The scene is the same as before, Scene I, except that Gowan Stevens now sits in the chair behind the desk where the Governor had been sitting, and the Governor is no longer in the room. Temple now kneels before the desk, facing it, her arms on the desk and her face buried in her arms. Stevens now stands beside and over her. The hands of the clock show nine minutes past three.

Temple does not know that the Governor has gone and that her husband is now in the room.

TEMPLE (*her face still hidden*)
    And that's all. The police came, and the murdress still
    sitting in a chair in the kitchen in the dark, saying 'Yes,
    Lord, I done it', and then in the cell at the jail still say-
    ing it——
            (*Stevens leans and touches her arm, as if to
            help her up. She resists, though still not raising
            her head*)
    Not yet. It's my cue to stay down here until his honor
    or excellency grants our plea, isn't it? Or have I already
    missed my cue forever even if the sovereign state
    should offer me a handkerchief right out of its own
    elected public suffrage dressing-gown pocket? Because
    see?
            (*she raises her face, quite blindly, tearless, still
            not looking toward the chair where she could*)

> *see Gowan instead of the Governor, into the*
> *full glare of the light)*

Still no tears.

STEVENS

Get up, Temple.
> *(he starts to lift her again, but before he can do*
> *so, she rises herself, standing, her face still*
> *turned away from the desk, still blind; she puts*
> *her arm up almost in the gesture of a little girl*
> *about to cry, but instead she merely shields her*
> *eyes from the light while her pupils readjust)*

TEMPLE

Nor cigarette either; this time it certainly wont take
long, since all you have to say is, No.
> *(still not turning her face to look, even though*
> *she is now speaking directly to the Governor*
> *whom she still thinks is sitting behind the desk)*

Because you aren't going to save her, are you? Because
all this was not for the sake of her soul because her soul
doesn't need it, but for mine.

STEVENS (*gently*)

Why not finish first? Tell the rest of it. You had started
to say something about the jail.

TEMPLE

The jail. They had the funeral the next day—Gowan
had barely reached New Orleans, so he chartered an
airplane back that morning—and in Jefferson, everything going to the graveyard passes the jail, or going
anywhere else for that matter, passing right under the

upstairs barred windows—the bullpen and the cells where the Negro prisoners—the crapshooters and whiskey-peddlers and vagrants and the murderers and murdresses too—can look down and enjoy it, enjoy the funerals too. Like this. Some white person you know is in a jail or a hospital, and right off you say, How ghastly: not at the shame or the pain, but the walls, the locks, and before you even know it, you have sent them books to read, cards, puzzles to play with. But not Negroes. You dont even think about the cards and puzzles and books. And so all of a sudden you find out with a kind of terror, that they have not only escaped having to read, they have escaped having to escape. So whenever you pass the jail, you can see them—no, not them, you dont see them at all, you just see the hands among the bars of the windows, not tapping or fidgeting or even holding, gripping the bars like white hands would be, but just lying there among the interstices, not just at rest, but even restful, already shaped and easy and unanguished to the handles of the plows and axes and hoes, and the mops and brooms and the rockers of white folks' cradles, until even the steel bars fitted them too without alarm or anguish. You see? not gnarled and twisted with work at all, but even limbered and suppled by it, smoothed and even softened, as though with only the penny-change of simple sweat they had already got the same thing the white ones have to pay dollars by the ounce jar for. Not immune to work, and in compromise with work is not the right word either, but in confederacy with work and so free from it; in armistice, peace;—the same long supple hands serene and immune to anguish, so that all the owners of them need to look out with, to see with—to look out at the out-

doors—the funerals, the passing, the people, the freedom, the sunlight, the free air—are just the hands: not
the eyes: just the hands lying there among the bars and
looking out, that can see the shape of the plow or hoe
or axe before daylight comes; and even in the dark,
without even having to turn on the light, can not only
find the child, the baby—not her child but yours, the
white one—but the trouble and discomfort too—the
hunger, the wet didy, the unfastened safety-pin—and
see to remedy it. You see. If I could just cry. There was
another one, a man this time, before my time in Jefferson but Uncle Gavin will remember this too. His
wife had just died—they had been married only two
weeks—and he buried her and so at first he tried just
walking the country roads at night for exhaustion and
sleep, only that failed and then he tried getting drunk
so he could sleep, and that failed and then he tried
fighting and then he cut a white man's throat with a
razor in a dice game and so at last he could sleep for a
little while; which was where the sheriff found him,
asleep on the wooden floor of the gallery of the house
he had rented for his wife, his marriage, his life, his old
age. Only that waked him up, and so in the jail that afternoon, all of a sudden it took the jailer and a deputy
and five other Negro prisoners just to throw him down
and hold him while they locked the chains on him;—
lying there on the floor with more than a half dozen
men panting to hold him down, and what do you think
he said? 'Look like I just cant quit thinking. Look like I
just cant quit.'

     (*she ceases, blinking, rubs her eyes and then ex-
     tends one hand blindly toward Stevens, who
     has already shaken out his handkerchief and*

*hands it to her. There are still no tears on her
face; she merely takes the handkerchief and
dabs, pats at her eyes with it as if it were a
powder-puff, talking again)*

But we have passed the jail, haven't we? We're in the
courtroom now. It was the same there; Uncle Gavin
had rehearsed her, of course, which was easy, since all
you can say when they ask you to answer to a murder
charge is, Not Guilty. Otherwise, they cant even have
a trial; they would have to hurry out and find another
murderer before they could take the next official step.
So they asked her, all correct and formal among the
judges and lawyers and bailiffs and jury and the Scales
and the Sword and the flag and the ghosts of Coke
upon Littleton upon Bonaparte and Julius Caesar and
all the rest of it, not to mention the eyes and the faces
which were getting a moving picture show for free
since they had already paid for it in the taxes, and nobody really listening since there was only one thing
she could say. Except that she didn't say it: just raising
her head enough to be heard plain—not loud: just
plain—and said, 'Guilty, Lord' —— like that, disrupt-
ing and confounding and dispersing and flinging back
two thousand years, the whole edifice of corpus juris
and rules of evidence we have been working to make
stand up by itself ever since Caesar, like when without
even watching yourself or even knowing you were
doing it, you would reach out your hand and turn over
a chip and expose to air and light and vision the frantic and aghast turmoil of an antbed. And moved the
chip again, when even the ants must have thought
there couldn't be another one within her reach: when
they finally explained to her that to say she was not

guilty, had nothing to do with truth but only with law, and this time she said it right, Not Guilty, and so then the jury could tell her she lied and everything was all correct again and, as everybody thought, even safe, since now she wouldn't be asked to say anything at all anymore. Only, they were wrong; the jury said Guilty and the judge said Hang and now everybody was already picking up his hat to go home, when she picked up that chip too: the judge said, 'And may God have mercy on your soul' and Nancy answered: 'Yes, Lord.'

(*she turns suddenly, almost briskly, speaking so briskly that her momentum carries on past the instant when she sees and recognises Gowan sitting where she had thought all the time that the Governor was sitting and listening to her*)

And that is all, this time. And so now you can tell us. I know you're not going to save her, but now you can say so. It wont be difficult. Just one word——

(*she stops, arrested, utterly motionless, but even then she is first to recover*)

Oh God.

(*Gowan rises quickly. Temple whirls to Stevens*)

Why is it you must always believe in plants? Do you have to? Is it because you have to? Because you are a lawyer? No, I'm wrong. I'm sorry; I was the one that started us hiding gimmicks on each other, wasn't it?

(*quickly: turning to Gowan*)

Of course; you didn't take the sleeping pill at all. Which means you didn't even need to come here for the Governor to hide you behind the door or under the desk or wherever it was he was trying to tell me you were hiding and listening, because after all the governor of a southern state has got to try to act like he regrets having to aberrate from being a gentleman——

STEVENS (*to Temple*)
    Stop it.

GOWAN
    Maybe we both didn't start hiding soon enough—by
    about eight years—not in desk drawers either, but in
    two abandoned mine shafts, one in Siberia and the
    other at the South Pole, maybe.

TEMPLE
    All right. I didn't mean hiding. I'm sorry.

GOWAN
    Dont be. Just draw on your eight years' interest for that.
        (*to Stevens*)
    All right, all right; tell me to shut up too.
        (*to no one directly*)
    In fact, this may be the time for me to start saying sorry
    for the next eight-year term. Just give me a little time.
    Eight years of gratitude might be a habit a little hard to
    break. So here goes.
        (*to Temple*)
    I'm sorry. Forget it.

TEMPLE
    I would have told you.

GOWAN
    You did. Forget it. You see how easy it is? You could
    have been doing that yourself for eight years: every
    time I would say 'Say sorry, please', all you would need
    would be to answer: 'I did. Forget it.'
        (*to Stevens*)
    I guess that's all, isn't it? We can go home now.
        (*he starts to come around the desk*)

TEMPLE

Wait.

(*Gowan stops; they look at each other*)

Where are you going?

GOWAN

I said home, didn't I? To pick up Bucky and carry him back to his own bed again.

(*they look at one another*)

You're not even going to ask me where he is now?

(*answers himself*)

Where we always leave our children when the clutch ——

STEVENS (*to Gowan*)

Maybe I will say shut up this time.

GOWAN

Only let me finish first. I was going to say, 'with our handiest kinfolks.'

(*to Temple*)

I carried him to Maggie's.

STEVENS (*moving*)

I think we can all go now. Come on.

GOWAN

So do I.

(*he comes on around the desk, and stops again;
to Temple*)

Make up your mind. Do you want to ride with me, or Gavin?

STEVENS (*to Gowan*)

Go on. You can pick up Bucky.

GOWAN
Right.
>   (*he turns, starts toward the steps front, where
>   Temple and Stevens entered, then stops*)
That's right. I'm probably still supposed to use the spy's
entrance.
>   (*he turns back, starts around the desk again, to-
>   ward the door at rear, sees Temple's gloves and
>   bag on the desk, and takes them up and holds
>   them out to her: roughly almost*)
Here. This is what they call evidence; dont forget
these.
>   (*Temple takes the bag and gloves. Gowan goes
>   on toward the door at rear*)

TEMPLE (*after him*)
Did you have a hat and coat?
>   (*he doesn't answer. He goes on, exits*)
Oh God. Again.

STEVENS (*touches her arm*)
Come on.

TEMPLE (*not moving yet*)
Tomorrow and tomorrow and tomorrow——

STEVENS (*speaking her thought, finishing the sentence*)
—he will wreck the car again against the wrong tree, in
the wrong place, and you will have to forgive him again,
for the next eight years until he can wreck the car again
in the wrong place, against the wrong tree——

TEMPLE
I was driving it too. I was driving some of the time too.

STEVENS (*gently*)
   Then let that comfort you.
         (*he takes her arm again, turns her toward the
         stairs*)
   Come on. It's late.

TEMPLE (*holds back*)
   Wait. He said, No.

STEVENS
   Yes.

TEMPLE
   Did he say why?

STEVENS
   Yes. He cant.

TEMPLE
   Cant? The Governor of a state, with all the legal power
   to pardon or at least reprieve, cant?

STEVENS
   That's just law. If it was only law, I could have plead in-
   sanity for her at any time, without bringing you here at
   two oclock in the morning——

TEMPLE
   And the other parent too; dont forget that. I dont know
   yet how you did it . . . . Yes, Gowan was here first; he
   was just pretending to be asleep when I carried Bucky
   in and put him in his bed; yes, that was what you
   called that leaking valve, when we stopped at the fill-

ing station to change the wheel: to let him get ahead of
us——

STEVENS

All right. He wasn't even talking about justice. He was
talking about a child, a little boy——

TEMPLE

That's right. Make it good: the same little boy to hold
whose normal and natural home together, the murdress, the nigger, the dope-fiend whore, didn't hesitate
to cast the last gambit—and maybe that's the wrong
word too, isn't it?—she knew and had: her own debased and worthless life. Oh yes, I know that answer
too; that was brought out here tonight too: that a little
child shall not suffer in order to come unto Me. So
good can come out of evil.

STEVENS

It not only can, it must.

TEMPLE

So touché, then. Because what kind of natural and
normal home can that little boy have where his father
may at any time tell him he has no father?

STEVENS

Haven't you been answering that question every day
for eight years? Didn't Nancy answer it for you when
she told you how you had fought back, not for yourself, but for that little boy? Not to show the father that
he was wrong, nor even to prove to the little boy that
the father was wrong, but to let the little boy learn

with his own eyes that nothing, not even that, which could possibly enter that house, could ever harm him?

TEMPLE

But I quit. Nancy told you that too.

STEVENS

She doesn't think so now. Isn't that what she's going to prove Friday morning?

TEMPLE

Friday. The black day. The day you never start on a journey. Except that Nancy's journey didn't start at daylight or sunup or whenever it is polite and tactful to hang people, day after tomorrow. Her journey started that morning eight years ago when I got on the train at the University——

(*she stops: a moment; then quietly*)

Oh God, that was Friday too; that baseball game was Friday——

(*rapidly*)

You see? Dont you see? It's nowhere near enough yet. Of course he wouldn't save her. If he did that, it would be over: Gowan could just throw me out, which he may do yet, or I could throw Gowan out, which I could have done until it got too late now, too late forever now, or the judge could have thrown us both out and given Bucky to an orphanage, and it would be all over. But now it can go on, tomorrow and tomorrow and tomorrow, forever and forever and forever——

STEVENS (*gently tries to start her*)

Come on.

TEMPLE (*holding back*)

Tell me exactly what he did say. Not tonight: it couldn't have been tonight—or did he say it over the telephone, and we didn't even need——

STEVENS

He said it a week ago——

TEMPLE

Yes, about the same time when you sent the wire. What did he say?

STEVENS (*quotes*)

'Who am I, to have the brazen temerity and hardihood to set the puny appanage of my office in the balance against that simple undeviable aim? Who am I, to render null and abrogate the purchase she made with that poor crazed lost and worthless life?'

TEMPLE (*wildly*)

And good too—good and mellow too. So it was not even in hopes of saving her life, that I came here at two oclock in the morning. It wasn't even to be told that he had already decided not to save her. It was not even to confess to my husband, but to do it in the hearing of two strangers, something which I had spent eight years trying to expiate so that my husband wouldn't have to know about it. Dont you see? That's just suffering. Not for anything: just suffering.

STEVENS

You came here to affirm the very thing which Nancy is going to die tomorrow morning to postulate: that little children, as long as they are little children, shall be intact, unanguished, untorn, unterrified.

TEMPLE (*quietly*)
  All right. I have done that. Can we go home now?

STEVENS
  Yes.
        (*she turns, moves toward the steps, Stevens be-
        side her. As she reaches the first step, she falters,
        seems to stumble slightly, like a sleepwalker.
        Stevens steadies her, but at once she frees her
        arm, and begins to descend*)

TEMPLE (*on the first step: to no one, still with that sleep-
        walker air*)
  To save my soul—if I have a soul. If there is a God to
  save it—a God who wants it——

(*Curtain*)

ACT III

The Jail

So, although in a sense the jail was both older and less old than the courthouse, in actuality, in time, in observation and memory, it was older even than the town itself. Because there was no town until there was a courthouse, and no courthouse until (like some unsentient unweaned creature torn violently from the dug of its dam) the floorless lean-to rabbit-hutch housing the iron chest was reft from the log flank of the jail and transmogrified into a by-neo-Greek-out-of-Georgian-England edifice set in the center of what in time would be the town Square (as a result of which, the town itself had moved one block south—or rather, no town then and yet, the courthouse itself the catalyst: a mere dusty widening of the trace, trail, pathway in a forest of oak and ash and hickory and sycamore and flowering catalpa and dogwood and judas tree and per-simmon and wild plum, with on one side old Alec Holston's tavern and coaching-yard, and a little further along, Ratcliffe's trading-post-store and the blacksmith's, and diagonal to all of them, en face and solitary beyond the dust, the log jail; moved—the town—complete and intact, one block south-ward, so that now, a century and a quarter later, the coaching-yard and Ratcliffe's store were gone and old Alec's tavern and the blacksmith's were a hotel and a garage, on a main thor-oughfare true enough but still a business side-street, and the

jail across from them, though transformed also now into two
storeys of Georgian brick by the hand ((or anyway pocket-
books)) of Sartoris and Sutpen and Louis Grenier, faced not
even on a side-street but on an alley);

And so, being older than all, it had seen all: the mutation and
the change: and, in that sense, had recorded them (indeed, as
Gavin Stevens, the town lawyer and the county amateur
Cincinnatus, was wont to say, if you would peruse in unbroken—ay, overlapping—continuity the history of a community,
look not in the church registers and the courthouse records,
but beneath the successive layers of calsomine and creosote
and whitewash on the walls of the jail, since only in that
forcible carceration does man find the idleness in which to
compose, in the gross and simple terms of his gross and simple
lusts and yearnings, the gross and simple recapitulations of his
gross and simple heart); invisible and impacted, not only beneath the annual inside creosote-and-whitewash of bullpen
and cell, but on the blind outside walls too, first the simple
mud-chinked log ones and then the symmetric brick, not only
the scrawled illiterate repetitive unimaginative doggerel and
the perspectiveless almost prehistoric sexual picture-writing,
but the images, the panorama not only of the town but of its
days and years until a century and better had been accom-
plished, filled not only with its mutation and change from a
halting-place: to a community: to a settlement: to a village: to a
town, but with the shapes and motions, the gestures of passion
and hope and travail and endurance, of the men and women
and children in their successive overlapping generations long
after the subjects which had reflected the images were vanished and replaced and again replaced, as when you stand say
alone in a dim and empty room and believe, hypnotised beneath the vast weight of man's incredible and enduring *Was*,

that perhaps by turning your head aside you will see from the corner of your eye the turn of a moving limb—a gleam of crinoline, a laced wrist, perhaps even a Cavalier plume—who knows? provided there is will enough, perhaps even the face itself three hundred years after it was dust—the eyes, two jellied tears filled with arrogance and pride and satiety and knowledge of anguish and foreknowledge of death, saying no to death across twelve generations, asking still the old same unanswerable question three centuries after that which reflected them had learned that the answer didn't matter, or—better still—had forgotten the asking of it—in the shadowy fathomless dreamlike depths of an old mirror which has looked at too much too long;

But not in shadow, not this one, this mirror, these logs: squatting in the full glare of the stump-pocked clearing during those first summers, solitary on its side of the dusty widening marked with an occasional wheel but mostly by the prints of horses and men: Pettigrew's private pony express until he and it were replaced by a monthly stagecoach from Memphis, the race horse which Jason Compson traded to Ikkemotubbe, old Mohataha's son and the last ruling Chickasaw chief in that section, for a square of land so large that, as the first formal survey revealed, the new courthouse would have been only another of Compson's outbuildings had not the town Corporation bought enough of it (at Compson's price) to forefend themselves being trespassers, and the saddlemare which bore Doctor Habersham's worn black bag (and which drew the buggy after Doctor Habersham got too old and stiff to mount the saddle), and the mules which drew the wagon in which, seated in a rocking chair beneath a French parasol held by a Negro slave girl, old Mohataha would come to town on Saturdays (and came that last time to set her capital X on the paper which ratified the dis-

possession of her people forever, coming in the wagon that
time too, barefoot as always but in the purple silk dress which
her son, Ikkemotubbe, had brought her back from France, and
a hat crowned with the royal-colored plume of a queen, beneath the slave-held parasol still and with another female slave
child squatting on her other side holding the crusted slippers
which she had never been able to get her feet into, and in the
back of the wagon the petty rest of the unmarked Empire flot-
sam her son had brought to her which was small enough to be
moved; driving for the last time out of the woods into the dusty
widening before Ratcliffe's store where the Federal land agent
and his marshal waited for her with the paper, and stopped the
mules and sat for a little time, the young men of her body
guard squatting quietly about the halted wagon after the eight-
mile walk, while from the gallery of the store and of Holston's
tavern the settlement—the Ratcliffes and Compsons and Pea-
bodys and Pettigrews ((not Grenier and Holston and Habersham, because Louis Grenier declined to come in to see it,
and for the same reason old Alec Holston sat alone on that
hot afternoon before the smoldering log in the fireplace of his
taproom, and Doctor Habersham was dead and his son had
already departed for the West with his bride, who was Mohataha's grand-daughter, and his father-in-law, Mohataha's son,
Ikkemotubbe))—looked on, watched: the inscrutable ageless
wrinkled face, the fat shapeless body dressed in the cast-off
garments of a French queen, which on her looked like the Sunday costume of the madam of a rich Natchez or New Orleans
brothel, sitting in a battered wagon inside a squatting ring of
her household troops, her young men dressed in their Sunday
clothes for travelling too: then she said, 'Where is this Indian
territory?' And they told her: West. 'Turn the mules west,' she
said, and someone did so, and she took the pen from the agent
and made her X on the paper and handed the pen back and

the wagon moved, the young men rising too, and she vanished
so across that summer afternoon to that terrific and infinitesimal creak and creep of ungreased wheels, herself immobile
beneath the rigid parasol, grotesque and regal, bizarre and
moribund, like obsolescence's self riding off the stage on its
own obsolete catafalque, looking not once back, not once back
toward home);

But most of all, the prints of men—the fitted shoes which Doctor Habersham and Louis Grenier had brought from the Atlantic seaboard, the cavalry boots in which Alec Holston had
ridden behind Francis Marion, and—more myriad almost
than leaves, outnumbering all the others lumped together—
the moccasins, the deerhide sandals of the forest, worn not by
the Indians but by white men, the pioneers, the long hunters,
as though they had not only vanquished the wilderness but had
even stepped into the very footgear of them they dispossessed
(and mete and fitting so, since it was by means of his feet and
legs that the white man conquered America; the closed and
split U's of his horses and cattle overlay his own prints always,
merely consolidating his victory);—(the jail) watched them
all, red men and white and black—the pioneers, the hunters,
the forest men with rifles, who made the same light rapid
soundless toed-in almost heel-less prints as the red men they
dispossessed and who in fact dispossessed the red men for that
reason: not because of the grooved barrel but because they
could enter the red man's milieu and make the same footprints
that he made; the husbandman printing deep the hard heels of
his brogans because of the weight he bore on his shoulders: axe
and saw and plow-stock, who dispossessed the forest man for
the obverse reason: because with his saw and axe he simply removed, obliterated, the milieu in which alone the forest man
could exist; then the land speculators and the traders in slaves

and whiskey who followed the husbandmen, and the politicians who followed the land speculators, printing deeper and
deeper the dust of that dusty widening, until at last there was
no mark of Chickasaw left in it anymore; watching (the jail)
them all, from the first innocent days when Doctor Habersham and his son and Alec Holston and Louis Grenier were
first guests and then friends of Ikkemotubbe's Chicksaw clan;
then an Indian agent and a land-office and a trading-post, and
suddenly Ikkemotubbe and his Chickasaws were themselves
the guests without being friends of the federal government;
then Ratcliffe, and the trading-post was no longer simply an Indian trading-post, though Indians were still welcome, of course
(since, after all, they owned the land or anyway were on it first
and claimed it), then Compson with his race horse and
presently Compson began to own the Indian accounts for tobacco and calico and jeans pants and cooking-pots on Ratcliffe's books (in time he would own Ratcliffe's books too) and
one day Ikkemotubbe owned the race horse and Compson
owned the land itself, some of which the city fathers would
have to buy from him at his price in order to establish a town;
and Pettigrew with his tri-weekly mail, and then a monthly
stage and the new faces coming in faster than old Alec Holston, arthritic and irascible, hunkered like an old surly bear
over his smoldering hearth even in the heat of summer (he
alone now of that original three, since old Grenier no longer
came in to the settlement, and old Doctor Habersham was
dead, and the old Doctor's son, in the opinion of the settlement, had already turned Indian and renegade even at the age
of twelve or fourteen) any longer made any effort, wanted, to
associate names with; and now indeed the last moccasin print
vanished from that dusty widening, the last toed-in heel-less
light soft quick long-striding print pointing west for an instant,
then trodden from the sight and memory of man by a heavy

leather heel engaged not in the traffic of endurance and hardihood and survival, but in money,—taking with it (the print)
not only the moccasins but the deer-hide leggins and jerkin
too, because Ikkemotubbe's Chickasaws now wore eastern
factory-made jeans and shoes sold them on credit out of Ratcliffe's and Compson's general store, walking in to the settlement on the white man's Saturday, carrying the alien shoes
rolled neatly in the alien pants under their arms, to stop at the
bridge over Compson's creek long enough to bathe their legs
and feet before donning the pants and shoes, then coming on
to squat all day on the store gallery eating cheese and crackers
and peppermint candy (bought on credit too out of Compson's
and Ratcliffe's showcase) and now not only they but Habersham and Holston and Grenier too were there on sufferance,
anachronistic and alien, not really an annoyance yet but simply a discomfort;

Then they were gone; the jail watched that: the halted ungreased unpainted wagon, the span of underfed mules attached to it by fragments of eastern harness supplemented by
raw deer-hide thongs, the nine young men—the wild men,
tameless and proud, who even in their own generation's memory had been free and, in that of their fathers, the heirs of
kings—squatting about it, waiting, quiet and composed, not
even dressed in the ancient forest-softened deerskins of their
freedom but in the formal regalia of the white man's inexplic-
able ritualistic sabbaticals: broadcloth trousers and white shirts
with boiled-starch bosoms (because they were travelling now;
they would be visible to outworld, to strangers:—and carrying
the New England–made shoes under their arms too since the
distance would be long and walking was better barefoot), the
shirts collarless and cravatless true enough and with the tails
worn outside, but still board-rigid, gleaming, pristine, and in

the rocking chair in the wagon, beneath the slave-borne parasol, the fat shapeless old matriarch in the regal sweat-stained
purple silk and the plumed hat, barefoot too of course but,
being a queen, with another slave to carry her slippers, putting
her cross to the paper and then driving on, vanishing slowly
and terrifically to the slow and terrific creak and squeak of the
ungreased wagon—apparently and apparently only, since in
reality it was as though, instead of putting an inked cross at the
foot of a sheet of paper, she had lighted the train of a mine set
beneath a dam, a dyke, a barrier already straining, bulging, bel-
lying, not only towering over the land but leaning, looming,
imminent with collapse, so that it only required the single light
touch of the pen in that brown illiterate hand, and the wagon
did not vanish slowly and terrifically from the scene to the terrific sound of its ungreased wheels, but was swept, hurled,
flung not only out of Yoknapatawpha County and Mississippi
but the United States too, immobile and intact—the wagon,
the mules, the rigid shapeless old Indian woman and the nine
heads which surrounded her—like a float or a piece of stage
property dragged rapidly into the wings across the very back-
drop and amid the very bustle of the property-men setting up
for the next scene and act before the curtain had even had
time to fall;

There was no time; the next act and scene itself clearing its
own stage without waiting for property-men; or rather, not
even bothering to clear the stage but commencing the new act
and scene right in the midst of the phantoms, the fading
wraiths of that old time which had been exhausted, used up, to
be no more and never return: as though the mere and simple
orderly ordinary succession of days was not big enough, com-
prised not scope enough, and so weeks and months and years
had to be condensed and compounded into one burst, one

surge, one soundless roar filled with one word: town: city: with
a name: Jefferson; men's mouths and their incredulous faces
(faces to which old Alec Holston had long since ceased trying
to give names or, for that matter, even to recognise) were filled
with it; that was only yesterday, and by tomorrow the vast bright
rush and roar had swept the very town one block south, leaving
in the tideless backwater of an alley on a sidestreet the old jail
which, like the old mirror, had already looked at too much too
long, or like the patriarch who, whether or not he decreed the
conversion of the mud-chinked cabin into a mansion, had at
least foreseen it, is now not only content but even prefers the
old chair on the back gallery, free of the rustle of blue prints
and the uproar of bickering architects in the already dismantled living-room;

It (the old jail) didn't care, tideless in that backwash, insulated
by that city block of space from the turmoil of the town's
birthing, the mud-chinked log walls even carcerant of the flot-
sam of an older time already on its rapid way out too: an occasional runaway slave or drunken Indian or shoddy would-be
heir of the old tradition of Mason or Hare or Harpe (biding its
time until, the courthouse finished, the jail too would be trans-
lated into brick, but, unlike the courthouse, merely a veneer of
brick, the old mud-chinked logs of the ground floor still intact
behind the patterned and symmetric sheath); no longer even
watching now, merely cognizant, remembering: only yesterday
was a wilderness ordinary, a store, a smithy, and already today
was not a town, a city, but *the* town and city: named; not a
courthouse but *the* courthouse, rising surging like the fixed
blast of a rocket, not even finished yet but already looming,
beacon focus and lodestar, already taller than anything else,
out of the rapid and fading wilderness,—not the wilderness receding from the rich and arable fields as tide recedes, but

rather the fields themselves, rich and inexhaustible to the plow, rising sunward and airward out of swamp and morass, themselves thrusting back and down brake and thicket, bayou and bottom and forest, along with the copeless denizens—the wild men and animals—which once haunted them, wanting, dreaming, imagining, no other;—lodestar and pole, drawing the people—the men and women and children, the maidens, the marriageable girls and the young men, flowing, pouring in with their tools and goods and cattle and slaves and gold money, behind ox- or mule-teams, by steamboat up Ikkemotubbe's old river from the Mississippi; only yesterday Pettigrew's pony express had been displaced by a stage-coach, yet already there was talk of a railroad less than a hundred miles to the north, to run all the way from Memphis to the Atlantic Ocean;

Going fast now: only seven years, and not only was the courthouse finished, but the jail too: not a new jail of course but the old one veneered over with brick, into two storeys, with white trim and iron-barred windows: only its face lifted, because behind the veneer were still the old ineradicable bones, the old ineradicable remembering: the old logs immured intact and lightless between the tiered symmetric bricks and the whitewashed plaster, immune now even to having to look, see, watch that new time which in a few years more would not even remember that the old logs were there behind the brick or had ever been, an age from which the drunken Indian had vanished, leaving only the highwayman, who had wagered his liberty on his luck, and the runaway nigger who, having no freedom to stake, had wagered merely his milieu; that rapid, that fast: Sutpen's untameable Paris architect long since departed, vanished (one hoped) back to wherever it was he had made that aborted midnight try to regain and had been over-

taken and caught in the swamp, not (as the town knew now) by
Sutpen and Sutpen's wild West Indian headman and Sutpen's
bear hounds, nor even by Sutpen's destiny nor even by his (the
architect's) own, but by that of the town: the long invincible
arm of Progress itself reaching into that midnight swamp to
pluck him out of that bayed circle of dogs and naked Negroes
and pine torches, and stamped the town with him like a rubber
signature and then released him, not flung him away like a
squeezed-out tube of paint, but rather (inattentive too) merely
opening its fingers, its hand; stamping his (the architect's) im-
print not on just the courthouse and the jail, but on the whole
town, the flow and trickle of his bricks never even faltering, his
molds and kilns building the two churches and then that Female Academy a certificate from which, to a young woman of
North Mississippi or West Tennessee, would presently have the
same mystic significance as an invitation dated from Windsor
castle and signed by Queen Victoria would for a young female
from Long Island or Philadelphia;

That fast now: tomorrow, and the railroad did run unbroken
from Memphis to Carolina, the light-wheeled bulb-stacked
wood-burning engines shrieking among the swamps and cane-
brakes where bear and panther still lurked, and through the
open woods where browsing deer still drifted in pale bands like
unwinded smoke: because they—the wild animals, the beasts—
remained, they coped, they would endure; a day, and they
would flee, lumber, scuttle across the clearings already over-
taken and relinquished by the hawk-shaped shadows of mail
planes; they would endure, only the wild men were gone; indeed, tomorrow, and there would be grown men in Jefferson
who could not even remember a drunken Indian in the jail; another tomorrow—so quick, so rapid, so fast—and not even a
highwayman anymore of the old true sanguinary girt and tradi-

tion of Hare and Mason and the mad Harpes; even Murrell, their thrice-compounded heir and apotheosis, who had taken his heritage of simple rapacity and bloodlust and converted it into a bloody dream of outlaw-empire, was gone, finished, as obsolete as Alexander, checkmated and stripped not even by man but by Progress, by a pierceless front of middleclass morality, which refused him even the dignity of execution as a felon, but instead merely branded him on the hand like an Elizabethan pickpocket—until all that remained of the old days for the jail to incarcerate was the runaway slave, for his little hour more, his little minute yet while the time, the land, the nation, the American earth, whirled faster and faster toward the plunging precipice of its destiny;

That fast, that rapid: a commodity in the land now which until now had dealt first in Indians: then in acres and sections and boundaries:—an economy: Cotton: a king: omnipotent and omnipresent: a destiny of which (obvious now) the plow and the axe had been merely the tools; not plow and axe which had effaced the wilderness, but Cotton: petty globules of Motion weightless and myriad even in the hand of a child, incapable even of wadding a rifle, let alone of charging it, yet potent enough to sever the very taproots of oak and hickory and gum, leaving the acre-shading tops to wither and vanish in one single season beneath that fierce minted glare; not the rifle nor the plow which drove at last the bear and deer and panther into the last jungle fastnesses of the river bottoms, but Cotton; not the soaring cupola of the courthouse drawing people into the country, but that same white tide sweeping them in: that tender skim covering the winter's brown earth, burgeoning through spring and summer into September's white surf crashing against the flanks of gin and warehouse and ringing like bells on the marble counters of the banks: altering not just the

face of the land, but the complexion of the town too, creating
its own parasitic aristocracy not only behind the columned
porticoes of the plantation houses, but in the counting-rooms
of merchants and bankers and the sanctums of lawyers, and not
only these last, but finally nadir complete: the county offices
too: of sheriff and tax-collector and bailiff and turnkey and
clerk; doing overnight to the old jail what Sutpen's architect
with all his brick and iron smith-work, had not been able to ac-
complish,—the old jail which had been unavoidable, a necessity, like a public comfort-station, and which, like the public
comfort-station, was not ignored but simply by mutual con-
cord, not seen, not looked at, not named by its purpose and
aim, yet which to the older people of the town, in spite of
Sutpen's architect's facelifting, was still the old jail—now trans-
lated into an integer, a moveable pawn on the county's political board like the sheriff's star or the clerk's bond or the bailiff's
wand of office; converted indeed now, elevated (an apotheosis)
ten feet above the level of the town, so that the old buried log
walls now contained the living-quarters for the turnkey's family
and the kitchen from which his wife catered, at so much a
meal, to the city's and the county's prisoners—perquisite not
for work or capability for work, but for political fidelity and the
numerality of votable kin by blood or marriage;—a jailor or
turnkey, himself someone's cousin and with enough other
cousins and inlaws of his own to have assured the election of
sheriff or chancery- or circuit-clerk,—a failed farmer who was
not at all the victim of his time but on the contrary, was its master, since his inherited and inescapable incapacity to support
his family by his own efforts, had matched him with an era and
a land where government was founded on the working premise
of being primarily an asylum for ineptitude and indigence,
for the private business failures among your or your wife's
kin whom otherwise you yourself would have to support,—so

much his destiny's master that, in a land and time where a
man's survival depended not only on his ability to drive a
straight furrow and to fell a tree without maiming or destroying
himself, that fate had supplied to him one child: a frail anemic
girl with narrow workless hands lacking even the strength to
milk a cow, and then capped its own vanquishment and eternal
subjugation by the paradox of giving him for his patronymic
the designation of the vocation at which he was to fail: Farmer;
this was the incumbent, the turnkey, the jailor; the old tough
logs which had known Ikkemotubbe's drunken Chickasaws
and brawling teamsters and trappers and flatboatmen (and—
for that one short summer night—the four highwaymen, one
of whom might have been the murderer, Wiley Harpe), were
now the bower framing a window in which mused hour after
hour and day and month and year, the frail blonde girl not
only incapable of (or at least excused from) helping her
mother cook, but even of drying the dishes after her mother
(or father perhaps) washed them,—musing, not even waiting
for anyone or anything, as far as the town knew, not even pen-
sive, as far as the town knew: just musing amid her blonde
hair in the window facing the country town street, day after
day and month after month and—as the town remembered
it—year after year for what must have been three or four of
them, inscribing at some moment the fragile and indelible
signature of her meditation in one of the panes of it (the window): her frail and workless name, scratched by a diamond
ring in her frail and workless hand, and the date: *Cecilia
Farmer April 16th 1861;*

At which moment the destiny of the land, the nation, the
South, the State, the County, was already whirling into the
plunge of its precipice, not that the State and the South knew
it, because the first seconds of fall always seem like soar: a

weightless deliberation preliminary to a rush not downward but
upward, the falling body reversed during that second by transubstantiation into the upward rush of earth; a soar, an apex, the
South's own apotheosis of its destiny and its pride, Mississippi
and Yoknapatawpha County not last in this, Mississippi among
the first of the eleven to ratify secession, the regiment of infantry
which John Sartoris raised and organised with Jefferson for its
headquarters, going to Virginia numbered Two in the roster of
Mississippi regiments, the jail watching that too but just by cog-
nizance from a block away: that noon, the regiment not even a
regiment yet but merely a voluntary association of untried men
who knew they were ignorant and hoped they were brave, the
four sides of the Square lined with their fathers or grandfathers
and their mothers and wives and sisters and sweethearts, the
only uniform present yet that one in which Sartoris stood with
his virgin sabre and his pristine colonel's braid on the courthouse balcony, bareheaded too while the Baptist minister
prayed and the Richmond mustering officer swore the regiment
in; and then (the regiment) gone; and now not only the jail but
the town too hung without motion in a tideless backwash: the
plunging body advanced far enough now into space as to have
lost all sense of motion, weightless and immobile upon the light
pressure of invisible air, gone now all diminishment of the
precipice's lip, all increment of the vast increaseless earth: a
town of old men and women and children and an occasional
wounded soldier (John Sartoris himself, deposed from his
colonelcy by a regimental election after Second Manassas,
came home and oversaw the making and harvesting of a crop
on his plantation before he got bored and gathered up a small
gang of irregular cavalry and carried it up into Tennessee to join
Forrest), static in quo, rumored, murmured of war only as from
a great and incredible dreamy distance, like far summer thunder: until the spring of '64, the once-vast fixed impalpable in-

creaseless and threatless earth now one omnivorous roar of rock
(a roar so vast and so spewing, flinging ahead of itself, like the
spray above the maelstrom, the preliminary anesthetic of shock
so that the agony of bone and flesh will not even be felt, as to
contain and sweep along with it the beginning, the first
ephemeral phase, of this story, permitting it to boil for an instant
to the surface like a chip or a twig—a match-stick or a bubble
say, too weightless to give resistance for destruction to function
against: in this case, a bubble, a minute globule which was its
own impunity, since what it—the bubble—contained, having
no part in rationality and being contemptuous of fact, was immune even to the rationality of rock)—a sudden battle center-
ing around Colonel Sartoris's plantation house four miles to the
north, the line of a creek held long enough for the main Confederate body to pass through Jefferson to a stronger line on the
river heights south of the town, a rear-guard action of cavalry in
the streets of the town itself (and this was the story, the beginning of it; all of it too, the town might have been justified in
thinking, presuming they had had time to see, notice, remark
and then remember, even that little)—the rattle and burst of
pistols, the hooves, the dust, the rush and scurry of a handful of
horsemen led by a lieutenant, up the street past the jail, and the
two of them—the frail and useless girl musing in the blonde
mist of her hair beside the window-pane where three or four (or
whatever it was) years ago she had inscribed with her grandmother's diamond ring her paradoxical and significantless
name (and where, so it seemed to the town, she had been standing ever since), and the soldier gaunt and tattered, battle-
grimed and fleeing and undefeated, looking at one another for
that moment across the fury and pell mell of battle;

Then gone; that night the town was occupied by Federal
troops; two nights later, it was on fire (the Square, the stores

and shops and the professional offices), gutted (the courthouse too), the blackened jagged topless jumbles of brick wall enclosing like a ruined jaw the blackened shell of the courthouse between its two rows of topless columns, which (the columns) were only blackened and stained, being tougher than fire: but not the jail, it escaped, untouched, insulated by its windless backwater from fire; and now the town was as though insulated by fire or perhaps cauterised by fire from fury and turmoil, the long roar of the rushing omnivorous rock fading on to the east with the fading uproar of the battle: and so in effect it was a whole year in advance of Appomattox (only the undefeated undefeatable women, vulnerable only to death, resisted, endured, irreconciliable); already, before there was a name for them (already their prototype before they even existed as a species), there were carpetbaggers in Jefferson—a Missourian named Redmond, a cotton- and quartermaster-supplies-speculator, who had followed the Northern army to Memphis in '61 and (nobody knew exactly how or why) had been with (or at least on the fringe of) the military household of the brigadier commanding the force which occupied Jefferson, himself— Redmond—going no further, stopping, staying, none knew the why for that either, why he elected Jefferson, chose that alien fire-gutted site (himself one, or at least the associate, of them who had set the match) to be his future home; and a German private, a blacksmith, a deserter from a Pennsylvania regiment, who appeared in the summer of '64, riding a mule, with (so the tale told later, when his family of daughters had become matriarchs and grandmothers of the town's new aristocracy) for saddle-blanket sheaf on sheaf of virgin and uncut United States banknotes, so Jefferson and Yoknapatawpha County had mounted Golgotha and passed beyond Appomattox a full year in advance, with returned soldiers in the town, not only the wounded from the battle of Jefferson, but whole men: not only

the furloughed from Forrest in Alabama and Johnston in Geor-
gia and Lee in Virginia, but the stragglers, the unmaimed flot-
sam and refuse of that single battle now drawing its final
constricting loop from the Atlantic Ocean at Old Point Comfort, to Richmond: to Chattanooga: to Atlanta: to the Atlantic
Ocean again at Charleston, who were not deserters but who
could not rejoin any still-intact Confederate unit for the reason
that there were enemy armies between, so that in the almost
faded twilight of that land, the knell of Appomattox made no
sound; when in the spring and early summer of '65 the for-
mally and officially paroled and disbanded soldiers began to
trickle back into the county, there was anticlimax; they returned to a land which not only had passed through Appomattox over a year ago, it had had that year in which to assimilate
it, that whole year in which not only to ingest surrender but
(begging the metaphor, the figure) to convert, metabolise it,
and then defecate it as fertilizer for the four-years' fallow land
they were already in train to rehabilitate a year before the Virginia knell rang the formal change, the men of '65 returning to
find themselves alien in the very land they had been bred and
born in and had fought for four years to defend, to find a working and already solvent economy based on the premise that it
could get along without them; (and now the rest of this story,
since it occurs, happens, here: not yet June in '65; this one had
indeed wasted no time getting back: a stranger, alone; the town
did not even know it had ever seen him before, because the
other time was a year ago and had lasted only while he gal-
loped through it firing a pistol backward at a Yankee army, and
he had been riding a horse—a fine though a little too small
and too delicate blooded mare—where now he rode a big
mule, which for that reason—its size—was a better mule than
the horse was a horse, but it was still a mule, and of course the
town could not know that he had swapped the mare for the

mule on the same day that he traded his lieutenant's sabre — he still had the pistol — for the stocking full of seed corn he had seen growing in a Pennsylvania field and had not let even the mule have one mouthful of it during the long journey across the ruined land between the Atlantic seaboard and the Jefferson jail, riding up to the jail at last, still gaunt and tattered and dirty and still undefeated and not fleeing now but instead making or at least planning a single-handed assault against what any rational man would have considered insurmountable odds ((but then, that bubble had ever been immune to the ephemerae of facts)); perhaps, probably — without doubt: apparently she had been standing leaning musing in it for three or four years in 1864; nothing had happened since, not in a land which had even anticipated Appomattox, capable of shaking a meditation that rooted, that durable, that veteran — the girl watched him get down and tie the mule to the fence, and perhaps while he walked from the fence to the door he even looked for a moment at her, though possibly, perhaps even probably, not, since she was not his immediate object now, he was not really concerned with her at the moment, because he had so little time, he had none, really: still to reach Alabama and the small hill farm which had been his father's and would now be his, if — no, when — he could get there, and it had not been ruined by four years of war and neglect, and even if the land was still plantable, even if he could start planting the stocking of corn tomorrow, he would be weeks and even months late; during that walk to the door and as he lifted his hand to knock on it, he must have thought with a kind of weary and indomitable outrage of how, already months late, he must still waste a day or maybe even two or three of them before he could load the girl onto the mule behind him and head at last for Alabama, — this, at a time when of all things he would require patience and a clear head, trying for them ((courtesy too,

which would be demanded now)), patient and urgent and polite, undefeated, trying to explain, in terms which they could
understand or at least accept, his simple need and the urgency
of it, to the mother and father whom he had never seen before
and whom he never intended, or anyway anticipated, to see
again, not that he had anything for or against them either: he
simply intended to be too busy for the rest of his life, once they
could get on the mule and start for home; not seeing the girl
then, during the interview, not even asking to see her for a moment when the interview was over, because he had to get the
license now and then find the preacher: so that the first word
he ever spoke to her was a promise delivered through a
stranger; it was probably not until they were on the mule—the
frail useless hands whose only strength seemed to be that sufficient to fold the wedding license into the bosom of her dress
and then cling to the belt around his waist—that he looked at
her again or ((both of them)) had time to learn one another's
middle name);

That was the story, the incident, ephemeral of an afternoon in
late May, unrecorded by the town and the county because they
had little time too: which (the county and the town) had anticipated Appomattox and kept that lead, so that in effect Appomattox itself never overhauled them; it was the long pull of
course, but they had—as they would realise later—that price-
less, that unmatchable year; on New Year's Day, 1865, while
the rest of the South sat staring at the northeast horizon beyond which Richmond lay, like a family staring at the closed
door to a sick-room, Yoknapatawpha County was already nine
months gone in reconstruction; by New Year's of '66, the gutted walls (the rain of two winters had washed them clean of the
smoke and soot) of the Square had been temporarily roofed
and were stores and shops and offices again, and they had

begun to restore the courthouse: not temporary, this, but restored, exactly as it had been, between the two columned porticoes, one north and one south, which had been tougher than
dynamite and fire, because it was the symbol: the County and
the City: and they knew how, who had done it before; Colonel
Sartoris was home now, and General Compson, the first Jason's son, and though a tragedy had happened to Sutpen and
his pride—a failure not of his pride nor even of his own bones
and flesh, but of the lesser bones and flesh which he had believed capable of supporting the edifice of his dream—they
still had the old plans of his architect and even the architect's
molds, and even more: money, (strangely, curiously) Redmond, the town's domesticated carpet-bagger, symbol of a
blind rapacity almost like a biological instinct, destined to
cover the South like a migration of locusts; in the case of this
man, arriving a full year before its time and now devoting no
small portion of the fruit of his rapacity to restoring the very
building the destruction of which had rung up the curtain for
his appearance on the stage, had been the formal visa on his
passport to pillage; and by New Year's of '76, this same Redmond with his money and Colonel Sartoris and General
Compson had built a railroad from Jefferson north into Tennessee to connect with the one from Memphis to the Atlantic
Ocean; nor content there either, north or south: another ten
years (Sartoris and Redmond and Compson quarrelled, and
Sartoris and Redmond bought—probably with Redmond's
money—Compson's interest in the railroad, and the next year
Sartoris and Redmond had quarrelled and the year after that,
because of simple physical fear, Redmond killed Sartoris from
ambush on the Jefferson Square and fled, and at last even Sartoris's supporters—he had no friends: only enemies and frantic
admirers—began to understand the result of that regimental
election in the fall of '62) and the railroad was a part of that sys-

tem covering the whole South and East like the veins in an oak
leaf and itself mutually adjunctive to the other intricate sys-
tems covering the rest of the United States, so that you could
get on a train in Jefferson now and, by changing and waiting a
few times, go anywhere in North America;

No more into the United States, but into the *rest* of the United
States, because the long pull was over now; only the aging
unvanquished women were unreconciled, irreconciliable, reversed and irrevocably reverted against the whole moving una-
nimity of panorama until, old unordered vacant pilings above
a tide's flood, they themselves had an illusion of motion, facing
irreconciliably backward toward the old lost battles, the old
aborted cause, the old four ruined years whose very physical
scars ten and twenty and twenty-five changes of season had an-
nealed back into the earth; twenty-five and then thirty-five
years; not only a century and an age, but a way of thinking
died; the town itself wrote the epilogue and epitaph: 1900, on
Confederate Decoration Day, Mrs Virginia DuPre, Colonel
Sartoris's sister, twitched a lanyard and the spring-restive
bunting collapsed and flowed, leaving the marble effigy—the
stone infantryman on his stone pedestal on the exact spot
where forty years ago the Richmond officer and the local Baptist minister had mustered in the Colonel's regiment, and the
old men in the gray and braided coats (all officers now, none
less in rank than captain) tottered into the sunlight and fired
shotguns at the bland sky and raised their cracked quavering
voices in the shrill hackle-lifting yelling which Lee and Jackson and Longstreet and the two Johnstons (and Grant and
Sherman and Hooker and Pope and McClellan and Burnside
too for the matter of that) had listened to amid the smoke and
the din; epilogue and epitaph, because apparently neither the
U.D.C. ladies who instigated and bought the monument, nor

the architect who designed it nor the masons who erected it, had noticed that the marble eyes under the shading marble palm stared not toward the north and the enemy, but toward the south, toward (if anything) his own rear,—looking perhaps, the wits said (could say now, with the old war thirty-five years past and you could even joke about it—except the women, the ladies, the unsurrendered, the irreconciliable, who even after another thirty-five years would still get up and stalk out of picture houses showing *Gone With the Wind*), for reinforcements; or perhaps not a combat soldier at all, but a provost marshal's man looking for deserters, or perhaps himself for a safe place to run to: because that old war was dead; the sons of those tottering old men in gray had already died in blue coats in Cuba, the macabre mementos and testimonials and shrines of the new war already usurping the earth before the blasts of blank shotgun shells and the weightless collapsing of bunting had unveiled the final ones to the old;

Not only a new century and a new way of thinking, but of acting and behaving too: now you could go to bed in a train in Jefferson and wake up tomorrow morning in New Orleans or Chicago; there were electric lights and running water in almost every house in town except the cabins of Negroes; and now the town bought and brought from a great distance a kind of gray crushed ballast-stone called macadam, and paved the entire street between the depot and the hotel, so that no more would the train-meeting hacks filled with drummers and lawyers and court-witnesses need to lurch and heave and strain through the winter mud-holes; every morning a wagon came to your very door with artificial ice and put it in your icebox on the back gallery for you, the children in rotational neighborhood gangs following it (the wagon), eating the fragments of ice which the Negro driver chipped off for them; and that sum-

mer a specially-built sprinkling-cart began to make the round
of the streets each day; a new time, a new age: there were
screens in windows now; people (white people) could actually
sleep in summer night air, finding it harmless, uninimical: as
though there had waked suddenly in man (or anyway in his
womenfolks) a belief in his inalienable civil right to be free of
dust and bugs;

Moving faster and faster: from the speed of two horses on either
side of a polished tongue, to that of thirty then fifty then a hundred under a tin bonnet no bigger than a washtub: which from
almost the first explosion, would have to be controlled by
police; already in a back yard on the edge of town, an ex
blacksmith's-apprentice, a grease-covered man with the eyes of
a visionary monk, was building a gasoline buggy, casting and
boring his own cylinders and rods and cams, inventing his own
coils and plugs and valves as he found he needed them, which
would run, and did: crept popping and stinking out of the alley
at the exact moment when the banker Bayard Sartoris, the
Colonel's son, passed in his carriage: as a result of which, there
is on the books of Jefferson today a law prohibiting the opera-
tion of any mechanically-propelled vehicle on the streets of the
corporate town: who (the same banker Sartoris) died in one
(such was progress, that fast, that rapid) lost from control on an
icy road by his (the banker's) grandson, who had just returned
from (such was progress) two years of service as a combat air-
man on the Western Front and now the camouflage paint is
weathering slowly from a French point-seventy-five field piece
squatting on one flank of the base of the Confederate monument, but even before it faded there was neon in the town and
A.A.A. and C.C.C. in the county, and W.P.A. ("and XYZ and
etc.," as "Uncle Pete" Gombault, a lean clean tobacco-
chewing old man, incumbent of a political sinecure under the

designation of United States marshal—an office held back in
reconstruction times, when the State of Mississippi was a
United States military district, by a Negro man who was still
living in 1925—fire-maker, sweeper, janitor and furnace-
attendant to five or six lawyers and doctors and one of the
banks—and still known as "Mulberry" from the avocation
which he had followed before and during and after his incumbency as marshal: peddling illicit whiskey in pint and half-pint
bottles from a cache beneath the roots of a big mulberry tree
behind the drugstore of his pre-1865 owner—put it) in both;
W.P.A. and XYZ marking the town and the county as war itself
had not: gone now were the last of the forest trees which had
followed the shape of the Square, shading the unbroken
second-storey balcony onto which the lawyers' and doctors' offices had opened, which shaded in its turn the fronts of the
stores and the walkway beneath; and now was gone even the
balcony itself with its wrought-iron balustrade on which in
the long summer afternoons the lawyers would prop their feet
to talk; and the continuous iron chain looping from wooden
post to post along the circumference of the courthouse yard,
for the farmers to hitch their teams to; and the public watering
trough where they could water them, because gone was the last
wagon to stand on the Square during the spring and summer
and fall Saturdays and trading-days, and not only the Square
but the streets leading into it were paved now, with fixed signs
of interdiction and admonition applicable only to something
capable of moving faster than thirty miles an hour; and now the
last forest tree was gone from the courthouse yard too, replaced
by formal synthetic shrubs contrived and schooled in Wiscon-
sin greenhouses, and in the courthouse (the city hall too) a
courthouse and city hall gang, in miniature of course (but that
was not its fault but the fault of the city's and the county's
size and population and wealth) but based on the pattern of

Chicago and Kansas City and Boston and Philadelphia (and which, except for its minuscularity, neither Philadelphia nor Boston nor Kansas City nor Chicago need have blushed at) which every three or four years would try again to raze the old courthouse in order to build a new one, not that they did not like the old one nor wanted the new, but because the new one would bring into the town and county that much more increment of unearned federal money;

And now the paint is preparing to weather from an anti-tank howitzer squatting on rubber tires on the opposite flank of the Confederate monument; and gone now from the fronts of the stores are the old brick made of native clay in Sutpen's architect's old molds, replaced now by sheets of glass taller than a man and longer than a wagon and team, pressed intact in Pittsburgh factories and framing interiors bathed now in one shadowless corpse-glare of fluorescent light; and, now and at last, the last of silence too: the county's hollow inverted air one resonant boom and ululance of radio: and thus no more Yoknapatawpha's air nor even Mason and Dixon's air, but America's: the patter of comedians, the baritone screams of female vocalists, the babbling pressure to buy and buy and still buy arriving more instantaneous than light, two thousand miles from New York and Los Angeles; one air, one nation: the shadowless fluorescent corpse-glare bathing the sons and daughters of men and women, Negro and white both, who were born to and who passed all their lives in denim overalls and calico, haggling by cash or the installment-plan for garments copied last week out of *Harper's Bazaar* or *Esquire* in East Side sweat-shops: because an entire generation of farmers has vanished, not just from Yoknapatawpha's but from Mason and Dixon's earth: the self-consumer: the machine which displaced the man because the exodus of the man left no one to drive the mule, now that the machine was threatening to extinguish the mule; time was when the mule stood in droves at daylight in the plantation mule-lots across the plantation road from the serried identical ranks of two-room shotgun shacks in which lived in droves with his family the Negro tenant- or share- or furnish-hand who bridled him (the mule) in the lot at sunup and followed him through the plumb-straight monotony of identical furrows and back to the lot at sundown, with (the man) one eye on where the mule was going and the other eye on his (the mule's) heels; both gone now: the one, to the last of the forty- and fifty- and sixty-acre hill farms inaccessible from unmarked dirt roads, the other to New York and Detroit and Chicago and Los Angeles ghettos, or nine out of ten of him that is, the tenth one mounting from the handles of a plow to the springless bucket seat of a tractor, dispossessing and displacing the other nine just as the tractor had dispossessed and displaced the other eighteen mules to whom that nine would have been comple-ment; then Warsaw and Dunquerque displaced that tenth in his turn, and now the planter's not-yet-drafted son drove the tractor: and then Pearl Harbor and Tobruk and Utah Beach displaced that son, leaving the planter himself on the seat of the tractor, for a little while that is — or so he thought, forget-ting that victory or defeat both are bought at the same exorbi-tant price of change and alteration; one nation, one world: young men who had never been further from Yoknapatawpha County than Memphis or New Orleans (and that not often), now talked glibly of street intersections in Asiatic and Euro-pean capitals, returning no more to inherit the long monoto-nous endless unendable furrows of Mississippi cotton fields, living now (with now a wife and next year a wife and child and the year after that a wife and children) in automobile trailers or G.I. barracks on the outskirts of liberal arts colleges, and the fa-ther and now grandfather himself still driving the tractor across the gradually diminishing fields between the long looping skeins of electric lines bringing electric power from the Appalachian mountains, and the subterrene steel veins bringing the natural gas from the western plains, to the little lost lonely farmhouses glittering and gleaming with automatic stoves and washing machines and television antennae;

One nation: no longer anywhere, not even in Yoknapatawpha County, one last irreconciliable fastness of stronghold from which to enter the United States, because at last even the last old sapless indomitable unvanquished widow or maiden aunt had died and the old deathless Lost Cause had become a faded (though still select) social club or caste, or form of behavior when you remembered to observe it on the occasions when young men from Brooklyn, exchange students at Mississippi or Arkansas or Texas universities, vended tiny confederate battle flags among the thronged Saturday afternoon ramps of football stadia; one world: the tank gun: captured from a regiment of Germans in an African desert by a regiment of Japanese in American uniforms, whose mothers and fathers at the time were in a California detention camp for enemy aliens, and carried (the gun) seven thousand miles back to be set halfway between, as a sort of secondary flying buttress to a memento of Shiloh and The Wilderness; one universe, one cosmos: contained in one America: one towering frantic edifice poised like a card-house over the abyss of the mortgaged generations; one boom, one peace: one swirling rocket-roar filling the glittering zenith as with golden feathers, until the vast hollow sphere of his air, the vast and terrible burden beneath which he tries to stand erect and lift his battered and indomitable head—the very substance in which he lives and, lacking which, he would vanish in a matter of seconds—is murmurous with his fears and terrors and disclaimers and repudiations and his aspirations and dreams and his baseless hopes, bouncing back at him in radar waves from the constellations;

And still—the old jail—endured, sitting in its rumorless cul-de-sac, its almost seasonless backwater in the middle of that rush and roar of civic progress and social alteration and change like a collarless (and reasonably clean: merely dingy: with a day's stubble and no garters to his socks) old man sitting in his suspenders and stocking feet, on the back kitchen steps inside a walled courtyard; actually not isolated by location so much as insulated by obsolescence: on the way out of course (to disappear from the surface of the earth along with the rest of the town on the day when all America, after cutting down all the trees and levelling the hills and mountains with bulldozers, would have to move underground to make room for, get out of the way of, the motor cars) but like the track-walker in the tunnel, the thunder of the express mounting behind him, who finds himself opposite a niche or crack exactly his size in the wall's living and impregnable rock, and steps into it, inviolable and secure while destruction roars past and on and away, grooved ineluctably to the spidery rails of its destiny and destination; not even—the jail—worth selling to the United States for some matching allocation out of the federal treasury; not even (so fast, so far, was Progress) anymore a real pawn, let alone knight or rook, on the County's political board, not even plum in true worth of the word: simply a modest sinecure for the husband of someone's cousin, who had failed not as a father but merely as a fourth-rate farmer or day-laborer;

It survived, endured; it had its inevictable place in the town and the county; it was even still adding modestly not just to its but to the town's and the county's history too: somewhere behind that dingy brick facade, between the old durable hand-

molded brick and the cracked creosote-impregnated plaster of
the inside walls (though few in the town or county any longer
knew that they were there) were the old notched and morticed
logs which (this, the town and county did remember; it was
part of its legend) had held someone who might have been
Wiley Harpe; during that summer of 1864, the federal brigadier
who had fired the Square and the courthouse had used the jail
as his provost-marshal's guard-house; and even children in
high school remembered how the jail had been host to the
Governor of the State while he discharged a thirty-day sentence for contempt of court for refusing to testify in a paternity
suit brought against one of his lieutenants: but isolate, even its
legend and record and history, indisputable in authenticity yet
a little oblique, elliptic or perhaps just ellipsoid, washed thinly
over with a faint quiet cast of apocrypha: because there were
new people in the town now, strangers, outlanders, living in
new minute glass-walled houses set as neat and orderly and an-
tiseptic as cribs in a nursery ward, in new subdivisions named
Fairfield or Longwood or Halcyon Acres which had once been
the lawn or back yard or kitchen garden of the old residences
(the old obsolete columned houses still standing among them
like old horses surged suddenly out of slumber in the middle of
a flock of sheep), who had never seen the jail; that is, they had
looked at it in passing, they knew where it was, when their kin
or friends or acquaintances from the East or North or California visited them or passed through Jefferson on the way to New
Orleans or Florida, they could even repeat some of its legend
or history to them: but they had had no contact with it, it was
not a part of their lives; they had the automatic stoves and fur-
naces and milk deliveries and lawns the size of installment-
plan rugs; they had never had to go to the jail on the morning
after Juneteenth or July Fourth or Thanksgiving or Christmas
or New Year's (or for that matter, on almost any Monday morn-

ing) to pay the fine of houseman or gardener or handyman so that he could hurry on home (still wearing his hangover or his barely-stanched razor-slashes) and milk the cow or clean the furnace or mow the lawn;

So only the old citizens knew the jail anymore, not old people but old citizens: men and women old not in years but in the constancy of the town, or against that constancy, concordant (not coeval of course, the town's date was a century and a quarter ago now, but in accord against that continuation) with that thin durable continuity born a hundred and twenty-five years ago out of a handful of bandits captured by a drunken militia squad, and a bitter ironical incorruptible wilderness mail-rider, and a monster wrought-iron padlock,—that steadfast and durable and unhurryable continuity against or across which the vain and glittering ephemerae of progress and alteration washed in substanceless repetitive evanescent scarless waves, like the wash and glare of the neon sign on what was still known as the Holston House diagonally opposite, which would fade with each dawn from the old brick walls of the jail and leave no trace; only the old citizens still knew it: the intractable and obsolescent of the town who still insisted on wood-burning ranges and cows and vegetable gardens and handymen who had to be taken out of hock on the mornings after Saturday nights and holidays; or the ones who actually spent the Saturday- and holiday-nights inside the barred doors and windows of the cells or bullpen for drunkenness or fighting or gambling— the servants, housemen and gardeners and handymen, who would be extracted the next morning by their white folks, and the others (what the town knew as the New Negro, independent of that commodity) who would sleep there every night beneath the thin ruby checker-barred wash and fade of the hotel sign, while they worked their fines out on the street; and the

County, since its cattle-thieves and moonshiners went to trial from there, and its murderers—by electricity now (so fast, that fast, was Progress)—to eternity from there; in fact it was still, not a factor perhaps, but at least an integer, a cipher, in the county's political establishment; at least still used by the Board of Supervisors, if not as a lever, at least as something like Punch's stuffed club, not intended to break bones, not aimed to leave any permanent scars;

So only the old knew it, the irreconciliable Jeffersonians and Yoknapatawphians who had (and without doubt firmly intended to continue to have) actual personal dealings with it on the blue Monday mornings after holidays, or during the semi-yearly terms of Circuit or Federal Court:—until suddenly you, a stranger, an outlander say from the East or the North or the Far West, passing through the little town by simple accident, or perhaps relation or acquaintance or friend of one of the outland families which had moved into one of the pristine and recent subdivisions, yourself turning out of your way to fumble among road signs and filling stations out of frank curiosity, to try to learn, comprehend, understand what had brought your cousin or friend or acquaintance to elect to live here—not specifically here, of course, not specifically Jefferson, but such as here, such as Jefferson—, suddenly you would realise that something curious was happening or had happened here: that instead of dying off as they should as time passed, it was as though these old irreconciliables were actually increasing in number; as though with each interment of one, two more shared that vacancy: where in 1900, only thirty-five years afterward, there could not have been more than two or three capable of it, either by knowledge or memory of leisure, or even simple willingness and inclination, now, in 1951, eighty-six years afterward, they could be counted in dozens (and in 1965, a hundred years afterward, in hundreds because—by now you

had already begun to understand why your kin or friend or acquaintance had elected to come to such as this with his family
and call it his life—by then the children of that second outland
invasion following a war, would also have become not just Mis-
sissippians but Jeffersonians and Yoknapatawphians: by which
time—who knows?—not merely the pane, but the whole window, perhaps the entire wall, may have been removed and em-
balmed intact into a museum by an historical, or anyway a
cultural, club of ladies,—why, by that time, they may not even
know, or even need to know: only that the windowpane bearing the girl's name and the date is that old, which is enough;
has lasted that long: one small rectangle of wavy, crudely-
pressed, almost opaque glass, bearing a few faint scratches apparently no more durable than the thin dried slime left by the
passage of a snail, yet which has endured a hundred years) who
are capable and willing too to quit whatever they happen to be
doing—sitting on the last of the wooden benches beneath the
last of the locust and chinaberry trees among the potted
conifers of the new age dotting the courthouse yard, or in the
chairs along the shady sidewalk before the Holston House,
where a breeze always blows—to lead you across the street and
into the jail and (with courteous neighborly apologies to the
jailor's wife stirring or turning on the stove the peas and grits
and side-meat—purchased in bargain-lot quantities by shrewd
and indefatigable peditation from store to store—which she
will serve to the prisoners for dinner or supper at so much a
head—plate—payable by the County, which is no mean factor
in the sinecure of her husband's incumbency) into the kitchen
and so to the cloudy pane bearing the faint scratches which,
after a moment, you will descry to be a name and a date;

Not at first, of course, but after a moment, a second, because at
first you would be a little puzzled, a little impatient because of
your illness-at-ease from having been dragged without warning

or preparation into the private kitchen of a strange woman cooking a meal; you would think merely *What? So what?* annoyed and even a little outraged, until suddenly, even while you were thinking it, something has already happened: the faint frail meaningless even inference-less scratching on the ancient poor-quality glass you stare at, has moved, under your eyes, even while you stared at it, coalesced, seeming actually to have entered into another sense than vision: a scent, a whisper, filling that hot cramped strange room already fierce with the sound and reek of frying pork-fat: the two of them in conjunction—the old milky obsolete glass, and the scratches on it: that tender ownerless obsolete girl's name and the old dead date in April almost a century ago—speaking, murmuring, back from, out of, across from, a time as old as lavender, older than album or stereopticon, as old as daguerrotype itself;

And being a stranger and a guest would have been enough, since, a stranger and a guest, you would have shown the simple courtesy and politeness of asking the questions naturally expected of you by the host or anyway volunteer guide, who had dropped whatever he was doing (even if that had been no more than sitting with others of his like on a bench in a courthouse yard or on the sidewalk before a hotel) in order to bring you here; not to mention your own perfectly natural desire for, not revenge perhaps, but at least compensation, restitution, vindication, for the shock and annoyance of having been brought here without warning or preparation, into the private quarters of a strange woman engaged in something as intimate as cooking a meal; but by now you had not only already begun to understand why your kin or friend or acquaintance had elected, not Jefferson but such as Jefferson, for his life, but you had heard that voice, that whisper, murmur, frailer than the scent of lavender, yet (for that second anyway) louder than all the seethe and fury of frying fat; so you ask the questions, not only which are expected of you, but whose answers you yourself must have if you are to get back into your car and fumble with any attention and concentration among the road signs and filling stations, to get on to wherever it is you had started when you stopped by chance or accident in Jefferson for an hour or a day or a night, and the host—guide—answers them, to the best of his ability out of the town's composite heritage of remembering that long back, told, repeated, inherited to him by his father; or rather, his mother: from her mother: or better still, to him when he himself was a child, direct from his great-aunt: the spinsters, maiden and childless out of a time when there were too many women because too many of the young men were maimed or dead: the indomitable and undefeated, maiden progenitresses of spinster and childless descendants still capable of rising up and stalking out in the middle of *Gone With the Wind*;

And again one sense assumes the office of two or three: not only hearing, listening, and seeing too, but you are even standing on the same spot, the same boards she did that day she wrote her name into the window and on the other one three years later watching and hearing through and beyond that faint fragile defacement the sudden rush and thunder: the dust: the crackle and splatter of pistols: then the face, gaunt, battle-dirty, stubbled-over; urgent of course, but merely harried, harassed; not defeated, turned for a fleeing instant across the turmoil and the fury, then gone: and still the girl in the window (the guide—host—has never said one or the other; without doubt in the town's remembering after a hundred years it has changed that many times from blonde to dark and back to blonde again: which doesn't matter, since in your own remembering that tender mist and vail will be forever blonde) not even waiting: musing; a year, and still not even waiting: meditant, not even unimpatient: just patienceless, in the sense that blindness and zenith are colorless; until at last the mule, not out of the long northeastern panorama of defeat and dust and fading smoke, but drawn out of it by that impregnable, that invincible, that incredible, that terrifying passivity, coming at that one fatigueless unflagging jog all the way from Virginia,— the mule which was a better mule in 1865 than the blood mare had been a horse in '-2 and '-3 and '-4, for the reason that this was now 1865, and the man, still gaunt and undefeated: merely harried and urgent and short of time to get on to Alabama and see the condition of his farm—or (for that matter) if he still had a farm, and now the girl, the fragile and workless girl not only incapable of milking a cow but of whom it was never even de- manded, required, suggested, that she substitute for her father in drying the dishes, mounting pillion on a mule behind a paroled cavalry subaltern out of a surrendered army who had swapped his charger for a mule and the sabre of his rank and his defeatless pride for a stocking full of seed corn, whom she had not known or even spoken to long enough to have learned his middle name or his preference in food, or told him hers, and no time for that even now: riding, hurrying toward a coun- try she had never seen, to begin a life which was not even sim- ple frontier, engaged only with wilderness and shoeless savages and the tender hand of God, but one which had been ren- dered into a desert (assuming that it was still there at all to be returned to) by the iron and fire of civilization;

Which was all your host (guide) could tell you, since that was all he knew, inherited, inheritable from the town: which was enough, more than enough in fact, since all you needed was the face framed in its blonde and delicate vail behind the scratched glass; yourself, the stranger, the outlander from New

England or the prairies or the Pacific Coast, no longer come by the chance or accident of kin or friend or acquaintance or roadmap, but drawn too from ninety years away by that incredible and terrifying passivity, watching in your turn through and beyond that old milk-dim disfigured glass that shape, that delicate frail and useless bone and flesh departing pillion on a mule without one backward look, to the reclaiming of an abandoned and doubtless even ravaged (perhaps even usurped) Alabama hill farm,—being lifted onto the mule (the first time he touched her probably, except to put the ring on: not to prove nor even to feel, touch, if there actually was a girl under the calico and the shawls; there was no time for that yet; but simply to get her up so they could start), to ride a hundred miles to become the farmless mother of farmers (she would bear a dozen, all boys, herself no older, still fragile, still workless among the churns and stoves and brooms and stacks of wood which even a woman could split into kindlings; unchanged), bequeathing to them in their matronymic the heritage of that invincible inviolable ineptitude;

Then suddenly, you realise that that was nowhere near enough, not for that face;—bridehood, motherhood, grandmotherhood, then widowhood and at last the grave,—the long peaceful connubial progress toward matriarchy in a rocking chair nobody else was allowed to sit in, then a headstone in a country churchyard;—not for that passivity, that stasis, that invincible captaincy of soul which didn't even need to wait but simply to be, breathe tranquilly, and take food,—infinite not only in capacity but in scope too: that face, one maiden muse which had drawn a man out of the running pell mell of a cavalry battle, a whole year around the long iron perimeter of duty and oath, from Yoknapatawpha County, Mississippi, across Tennessee into Virginia and up to the fringe of Pennsylvania

before it curved back into its closing fade along the headwaters
of the Appomattox river and at last removed from him its iron
hand: where, a safe distance at last into the rainy woods from
the picket lines and the furled flags and the stacked muskets, a
handful of men leading spent horses, the still-warm pistols still
loose and quick for the hand in the unstrapped scabbards,
gathered in the failing twilight—privates and captains,
sergeants and corporals and subalterns—talking a little of one
last desperate cast southward where (by last report) Johnston
was still intact, knowing that they would not, that they were
done not only with vain resistance but with indominability too;
already departed this morning in fact for Texas, the West, New
Mexico: a new land even if not yet (spent too—like the
horses—from the long harassment and anguish of remaining
indomitable and undefeated) a new hope, putting behind
them for good and all the loss of both: the young dead bride;—
drawing him (that face) even back from this too, from no
longer having to remain undefeated too: who swapped the
charger for the mule and the sabre for the stocking of seed
corn: back across the whole ruined land and the whole disas-
trous year by that virgin inevictable passivity more inescapable
than lodestar;

Not that face; that was nowhere near enough: no symbol there
of connubial matriarchy, but fatal instead with all insatiate
and deathless sterility; spouseless, barren, and undescended;
not even demanding more than that: simply requiring it, requiring all,—Lilith's lost and insatiable face drawing the substance—the will and hope and dream and imagination—of
all men (you too: yourself and the host too) into that one
bright fragile net and snare; not even to be caught, over-flung,
by one single unerring cast of it, but drawn to watch in patient
and thronging turn the very weaving of the strangling golden

strands;—drawing the two of you from almost a hundred years away in your turn—yourself the stranger, the outlander from B.A. or (perhaps even) M.A. at Harvard or Northwestern or Stanford, passing through Jefferson by chance or accident on the way to somewhere else, and the host who in three generations has never been out of Yoknapatawpha further than a few prolonged Saturday nights in Memphis or New Orleans, who has heard of Jenny Lind, not because he has heard of Mark Twain and Mark Twain spoke well of her, but for the same reason that Mark Twain spoke well of her: not that she sang songs, but that she sang them in the old West in the old days, and the man sanctioned by public affirmation to wear a pistol openly in his belt is an inevictable part of the Missouri and the Yoknapatawpha dream too, but never of Duse or Bernhardt or Maximilian of Mexico, let alone whether the Emperor of Mexico even ever had a wife or not (saying—the host—: 'You mean, she was one of them? maybe even that emperor's wife?' and you: 'Why not? Wasn't she a Jefferson girl?')—to stand, in this hot strange little room furious with frying fat, among the roster and chronicle, the deathless murmur of the sublime and deathless names and the deathless faces, the faces omnivorous and insatiable and forever incontent: demon-nun and angel-witch; empress, siren, Erinys: Mistinguette too, invincibly possessed of a half-century more of years than the mere three score or so she bragged and boasted, for you to choose among, which one she was,—not *might* have been, nor even *could* have been, but *was*: so vast, so limitless in capacity is man's imagination to disperse and burn away the rubble-dross of fact and probability, leaving only truth and dream,—then gone, you are outside again, in the hot noon sun: late; you have already wasted too much time: to unfumble among the road signs and filling stations to get back onto a highway you know, back into the United

States; not that it matters since you know again now that there is no time: no space: no distance: a fragile and workless scratching almost depthless in a sheet of old barely transparent glass, and (all you had to do was look at it a while; all you have to do now is remember it) there is the clear undistanced voice as though out of the delicate antenna-skeins of radio, further than empress's throne, than splendid insatiation, even than matriarch's peaceful rocking chair, across the vast instantaneous intervention, from the long long time ago: '*Listen, stranger; this was myself: this was I*'.

SCENE I

Interior, the Jail. 10:30 A.M. March twelfth.

The common room, or 'bull-pen'. It is on the second floor. A heavy barred door at L is the entrance to it, to the entire cell-block, which — the cells — are indicated by a row of steel doors, each with its own individual small barred window, lining the right wall. A narrow passage at the far end of the right wall leads to more cells. A single big heavily-barred window in the rear wall looks down into the street. It is mid-morning of a sunny day.

The door, L, opens with a heavy clashing of the steel lock, and swings back and outward. Temple enters, followed by Stevens and the Jailor. Temple has changed her dress, but wears the fur coat and the same hat. Stevens is dressed exactly as he was in Act II. The Jailor is a typical small-town turnkey, in shirt-sleeves and no necktie, carrying the heavy keys on a big iron ring against his leg as a farmer carries a lantern, say. He is drawing the door to behind him as he enters.

Temple stops just inside the room. Stevens perforce stops also. The Jailor closes the door and locks it on the inside with another clash and clang of steel, and turns.

JAILOR

Well, Lawyer, singing school will be over after tonight, huh?

(to Temple)

You been away, you see. You dont know about this, you aint kept up with what's ——

> *(he stops himself quickly; he is about to commit what he would call a very bad impoliteness, what in the tenets of his class and kind would be the most grave of gaucherie and bad taste: referring directly to a recent bereavement in the presence of the bereaved, particularly one of this nature, even though by this time tomorrow the State itself will have made restitution with the perpetrator's life. He tries to rectify it)*

Not that I wouldn't too, if I'd a been the ma of the very ——

> *(stopping himself again; this is getting worse than ever; now he not only is looking at Stevens, but actually addressing him)*

Every Sunday night, and every night since last Sunday except last night—come to think of it, Lawyer, where was you last night? We missed you—Lawyer here and Na—the prisoner have been singing hymns in her cell. The first time, he just stood out there on the sidewalk while she stood in that window yonder. Which was all right, not doing no harm, just singing church hymns. Because all of us home folks here in Jefferson

and Yoknapatawpha County both know Lawyer
Stevens, even if some of us might have thought he got
a little out of line ——

> (*again it is getting out of hand; he realises it,
> but there is nothing he can do now; he is like
> someone walking a foot-log: all he can do is
> move as fast as he dares until he can reach solid
> ground or at least pass another log to leap to*)

defending a nigger murderer, let alone when it was his
own niece was mur ——

> (*and reaches another log and leaps to it with-
> out stopping: at least one running at right an-
> gles for a little distance into simple generality*)

—maybe suppose some stranger say, some durn Yankee
tourist, happened to be passing through in a car, when
we get enough durn criticism from Yankees like it is,—
besides, a white man standing out there in the cold,
while a durned nigger murderer is up here all warm and
comfortable; so it happened that me and Mrs Tubbs
hadn't went to prayer meeting that night, so we invited
him to come in; and to tell the truth, we come to enjoy
it too. Because as soon as they found out there wasn't
going to be no objection to it, the other nigger prisoners
(I got five more right now, but I taken them out back
and locked them up in the coal house so you could
have some privacy) joined in too, and by the second or
third Sunday night, folks was stopping along the street to
listen to them instead of going to regular church. Of
course, the other niggers would just be in and out over
Saturday and Sunday night for fighting or gambling or
vagrance or drunk, so just about the time they would
begin to get in tune, the whole choir would be a complete turn-over. In fact, I had a idea at one time to have

the Marshal comb the nigger dives and joints not for
drunks and gamblers, but basses and baritones.
>   (*he starts to laugh, guffaws once, then catches
>   himself; he looks at Temple with something al-
>   most gentle, almost articulate, in his face, taking
>   ((as though)) by the horns, facing frankly and
>   openly the dilemma of his own inescapable vice*)

Excuse me, Mrs Stevens. I talk too much. All I want to
say is, this whole county, not a man or woman, wife or
mother either in the whole state of Mississippi, that
dont—dont feel——
>   (*stopping again, looking at Temple*)

There I am, still at it, still talking too much. Wouldn't
you like for Mrs Tubbs to bring you up a cup of coffee
or maybe a coca cola? She's usually got a bottle or two
of sody pop in the icebox.

TEMPLE
>   No thank you, Mr Tubbs. If we could just see
>   Nancy——

JAILOR (*turning*)
>   Sure, sure.

He crosses toward the rear, R, and disappears into the passage.

TEMPLE
>   The blindfold again. Out of a coca cola bottle this
>   time or a cup of county-owned coffee.

Stevens takes the same pack of cigarettes from his overcoat
pocket, though Temple has declined before he can even offer
them.

TEMPLE

> No thanks. My hide's toughened now. I hardly feel it.
> People. They're really innately, inherently gentle and
> compassionate and kind. That's what wrings, wrenches
> . . . . something. Your entrails, maybe. The member
> of the mob who holds up the whole ceremony for
> seconds or even minutes while he dislodges a family of
> bugs or lizards from the log he is about to put on the
> fire ——
>> (*there is the clash of another steel door off-stage
>> as the Jailor unlocks Nancy's cell. Temple pauses,
>> turns and listens, then continues rapidly*)
> And now I've got to say 'I forgive you, sister' to the nig-
> ger who murdered my baby. No: it's worse: I've even
> got to transpose it, turn it around. I've got to start off
> my new life being forgiven again. How can I say that?
> Tell me. How can I?

She stops again and turns further as Nancy enters from the rear
alcove, followed by the Jailor, who passes Nancy and comes
on, carrying the ring of keys once more like a farmer's lantern.

JAILOR (*to Stevens*)

> Okay, Lawyer. How much time you want? Thirty min-
> utes? an hour?

STEVENS

> Thirty minutes should be enough.

JAILOR (*still moving toward the exit L*)

> Okay.
>> (*to Temple*)
> You sure you dont want that coffee or a coca cola? I
> could bring you up a rocking chair ——

TEMPLE

Thank you just the same, Mr Tubbs.

JAILOR

Okay.
(*at the exit door, unlocking it*)
Thirty minutes, then.

He unlocks the door, opens it, exits, closes and locks it behind him; the lock clashes, his footsteps die away. Nancy has slowed and stopped where the Jailor passed her; she now stands about six feet to the rear of Temple and Stevens. Her face is calm, unchanged. She is dressed exactly as before, except for the apron; she still wears the hat.

NANCY (*to Temple*)

You been to California, they tell me. I used to think maybe I would get there too, some day. But I waited too late to get around to it.

TEMPLE

So did I. Too late and too long. Too late when I went to California, and too late when I came back. That's it: too late and too long, not only for you, but for me too; already too late when both of us should have got around to running, like from death itself, from the very air anybody breathed named Drake or Mannigoe.

NANCY

Only, we didn't. And you come back, yesterday evening. I heard that too. And I know where you were last night, you and him both.
(*indicating Stevens*)
You went to see the Mayor.

TEMPLE

Oh God, the Mayor. No: the Governor, the Big Man himself, in Jackson. Of course; you knew that as soon as you realised that Mr Gavin wouldn't be here last night to help you sing, didn't you? In fact, the only thing you cant know about it, is what the Governor told us. You cant know that yet, no matter how clairvoyant you are, because we — the Governor and Mr Gavin and I — were not even talking about you; the reason I — we had to go and see him was not to beg or plead or bind or loose, but because it would be my right, my duty, my privilege —— Dont look at me, Nancy.

NANCY

I'm not looking at you. Besides, it's all right. I know what the Governor told you. Maybe I could have told you last night what he would say, and saved you the trip. Maybe I ought to have: — sent you the word as soon as I heard you were back home, and knowed what you and him ——

(*again she indicates Stevens with that barely discernible movement of her head, her hands still folded across her middle as though she still wore the absent apron*)

— both would probably be up to. Only, I didn't. But it's all right ——

TEMPLE

Why didn't you? Yes, look at me. This is worse, but the other is terrible.

NANCY

What?

TEMPLE

Why didn't you send me the word?

NANCY

Because that would have been hoping: the hardest thing of all to break, get rid of, let go of, the last thing of all poor sinning man will turn aloose. Maybe it's because that's all he's got. Leastways, he hold onto it, hangs onto it. Even with salvation laying right in his hand, and all he's got to do is, choose between it; even with salvation already in his hand and all he needs is just to shut his fingers, old sin is still too strong for him, and sometimes before he even knows it, he has throwed salvation away just grabbling back at hoping. But it's all right——

STEVENS

You mean, when you have salvation, you dont have hope?

NANCY

You dont even need it. All you need, all you have to do, is just believe. So maybe ——

STEVENS

Believe what?

NANCY

Just believe.—So maybe it's just as well that all I did last night, was just to guess where you all went. But I know now, and I know what the Big Man told you. And it's all right. I finished all that a long time back, that same day in the judge's court. No: before that

even: in the nursery that night, before I even lifted my
hand——

TEMPLE (*convulsively*)
Hush. Hush.

NANCY
All right. I've hushed. Because it's all right. I can get
low for Jesus too. I can get low for Him too.

TEMPLE
Hush! Hush! At least, dont blaspheme. But who am I,
to challenge the language you talk about Him in,
when He Himself certainly cant challenge it, since
that's the only language He arranged for you to learn?

NANCY
What's wrong with what I said? Jesus is a man too. He's
got to be. Menfolks listens to somebody because of
what he says. Women dont. They dont care what he
said. They listens because of what he is.

TEMPLE
Then let Him talk to me. I can get low for Him too, if
that's all He wants, demands, asks. I'll do anything He
wants if He'll just tell me what to do. No: how to do it.
I know what to do, what I must do, what I've got to do.
But how? We—I thought that all I would have to do
would be to come back and go to the Big Man and tell
him that it wasn't you who killed my baby, but I did it
eight years ago that day when I slipped out the back
door of that train, and that would be all. But we were
wrong. Then I—we thought that all it would be was,

for me just to come back here and tell you you had to die; to come all the way two thousand miles from California, to sit up all night driving to Jackson and talking for an hour or two and then driving back, to tell you you had to die; not just to bring you the news that you had to die, because any messenger could do that, but just so it could be me that would have to sit up all night and talk for the hour or two hours and then bring you the news back. You know: not to save you, that wasn't really concerned in it: but just for me, just for the suffering and the paying: a little more suffering simply because there was a little more time left for a little more of it, and we might as well use it since we were already paying for it; and that would be all, it would be finished then. But we were wrong again. That was all, only for you. You wouldn't be any worse off if I had never come back from California. You wouldn't even be any worse off. And this time tomorrow, you wont be anything at all. But not me. Because there's tomorrow, and tomorrow, and tomorrow. All you've got to do is, just to die. But let Him tell me what to do. No: that's wrong; I know what to do, what I'm going to do; I found that out that same night in the nursery too. But let Him tell me how. How? Tomorrow, and tomorrow, and still tomorrow. How?

NANCY

Trust in Him.

TEMPLE

Trust in Him. Look what He has already done to me. Which is all right; maybe I deserved it; at least I'm not the one to criticise or dictate to Him. But look what He did to you. Yet you can still say that. Why? Why? Is it because there isn't anything else?

NANCY

I dont know. But you got to trust Him. Maybe that's your pay for the suffering.

STEVENS

Whose suffering, and whose pay? Just each one's for his own?

NANCY

Everybody's. All suffering. All poor sinning man's.

STEVENS

The salvation of the world is in man's suffering. Is that it?

NANCY

Yes sir.

STEVENS

How?

NANCY

I dont know. Maybe when folks are suffering, they will be too busy to get into devilment, wont have time to worry and meddle one another.

TEMPLE

But why must it be suffering? He's omnipotent, or so they tell us. Why couldn't He have invented something else? Or, if it's got to be suffering, why cant it be just your own? why cant you buy back your own sins with your own agony? Why do you and my little baby both have to suffer just because I decided to go to a baseball game eight years ago? Do you have to suffer everybody else's anguish just to believe in God? What kind of God is it that has to blackmail His customers with the whole world's grief and ruin?

NANCY

He dont want you to suffer. He dont like suffering neither. But He cant help Himself. He's like a man that's got too many mules. All of a sudden one morning, he looks around and sees more mules than he can count at one time even, let alone find work for, and all he knows is that they are his, because at least dont nobody else want to claim them, and that the pasture fence was still holding them last night where they cant harm themselves nor nobody else the least possible. And that when Monday morning comes, he can walk in there and hem some of them up and even catch them if he's careful about not never turning his back on the ones he aint hemmed up. And that, once the gear is on them, they will do his work and do it good, only he's still got to be careful about getting too close to them, or forgetting that another one of them is behind him, even when he is feeding them. Even when it's Saturday noon again, and he is turning them back into the pasture, where even a mule can know it's got until Monday morning anyway to run free in mule sin and mule pleasure.

STEVENS

You have got to sin, too?

NANCY

You aint *got* to. You cant help it. And He knows that. But you can suffer. And He knows that too. He dont tell you not to sin, He just asks you not to. And He dont tell you to suffer. But He gives you the chance. He gives you the best He can think of, that you are capable of doing. And He will save you.

STEVENS

You too? a murdress? In heaven?

NANCY

I can work.

STEVENS

The harp, the raiment, the singing, may not be for Nancy Mannigoe—not now. But there's still the work to be done—the washing and sweeping, maybe even the children to be tended and fed and kept from hurt and harm and out from under the grown folks' feet?
    (*he pauses a moment. Nancy says nothing, im-
    mobile, looking at no one*)
Maybe even that baby?
    (*Nancy doesn't move, stir, not looking at any-
    thing apparently, her face still, bemused, expres-
    sionless*)
That one too, Nancy? Because you loved that baby, even at the very moment when you raised your hand against it, knew that there was nothing left but to raise your hand?
    (*Nancy doesn't answer nor stir*)
A heaven where that little child will remember noth-ing of your hands but gentleness because now this

earth will have been nothing but a dream that didn't matter? Is that it?

TEMPLE

Or maybe not that baby, not mine, because, since I destroyed mine myself when I slipped out the back end of that train that day eight years ago, I will need about all the forgiving and forgetting that one six-months-old baby is capable of. But the other one: yours: that you told me about, that you were carrying six months gone, and you went to the picnic or dance or frolic or fight or whatever it was, and the man kicked you in the stomach and you lost it? That one too?

STEVENS (*to Nancy*)

What? Its father kicked you in the stomach while you were pregnant?

NANCY

I dont know.

STEVENS

You dont know who kicked you?

NANCY

I know that. I thought you meant its pa.

STEVENS

You mean, the man who kicked you wasn't even its father?

NANCY

I dont know. Any of them might have been.

STEVENS

Any of them? You dont have any idea who its father was?

NANCY (*looks at Stevens impatiently*)

If you backed your behind into a buzz-saw, could you tell which tooth hit you first?
(*to Temple*)
What about that one?

TEMPLE

Will that one be there too, that never had a father and never was even born, to forgive you? Is there a heaven for it to go to so it can forgive you? Is there a heaven, Nancy?

NANCY

I dont know. I believes.

TEMPLE

Believe what?

NANCY

I dont know. But I believes.

They all pause at the sound of feet approaching beyond the exit door, all are looking at the door as the key clashes again in the lock and the door swings out and the Jailor enters, drawing the door to behind him.

JAILOR (*locking the door*)

Thirty minutes, Lawyer. You named it, you know: not me.

STEVENS
I'll come back later.

JAILOR (*turns and crosses toward them*)
Provided you dont put it off too late. What I mean, if you wait until tonight to come back, you might have some company; and if you put it off until tomorrow, you wont have no client.
(*to Nancy*)
I found that preacher you want. He'll be here about sundown, he said. He sounds like he might even be another good baritone. And you cant have too many, especially as after tonight you wont need none, huh? No hard feelings, Nancy. You committed about as horrible a crime as this county ever seen, but you're fixing to pay the law for it, and if the child's own mother——
(*he falters, almost pauses, catches himself and continues briskly, moving again*)
There, talking too much again. Come on, if Lawyer's through with you. You can start taking your time at daylight tomorrow morning, because you might have a long hard trip.

He passes her and goes briskly on toward the alcove at rear. Nancy turns to follow.

TEMPLE (*quickly*)
Nancy.
(*Nancy doesn't pause. Temple continues, rapidly*)
What about me? Even if there is one and somebody waiting in it to forgive me, there's still tomorrow and

tomorrow. And suppose tomorrow and tomorrow, and then nobody there, nobody waiting to forgive me ——

NANCY (*moving on after the Jailor*)
Believe.

TEMPLE
Believe what, Nancy? Tell me.

NANCY
Believe.

She exits into the alcove behind the Jailor. The steel door off-stage clangs, the key clashes. Then the Jailor reappears, approaches, and crosses toward the exit. He unlocks the door and opens it out again, pauses.

JAILOR
Yes sir. A long hard way. If I was ever fool enough to commit a killing that would get my neck into a noose, the last thing I would want to see would be a preacher. I'd a heap rather believe there wasn't nothing after death, than to risk the station where I was probably going to get off.
(*he waits, holding the door, looking back at them. Temple stands motionless until Stevens touches her arm slightly. Then she moves, stumbles slightly and infinitesimally, so infinitesimally and so quickly recovered that the Jailor has barely time to react to it, though he does so: with quick concern, with that quality about him almost gentle, almost articulate, turning from the door, even leaving it open as he starts quickly toward her*)

Here; you set down on the bench; I'll get you a glass of
water.
(*to Stevens*)
Durn it, Lawyer, why did you have to bring her——

TEMPLE (*recovered*)
I'm all right.

She walks steadily toward the door. The Jailor watches her.

JAILOR
You sure?

TEMPLE (*walking steadily and rapidly toward him and the
door now*)
Yes. Sure.

JAILOR (*turning back toward the door*)
Okay. I sure dont blame you. Durned if I see how even
a murdering nigger can stand this smell.

He passes on out the door and exits, invisible though still holding the door and waiting to lock it. Temple, followed by
Stevens, approaches the door.

JAILOR'S VOICE (*off-stage: surprised*)
Howdy. Gowan, here's your wife now.

TEMPLE (*walking*)
Anyone to save it. Anyone who wants it. If there is
none, I'm sunk. We all are. Doomed. Damned.

STEVENS (*walking*)
Of course we are. Hasn't He been telling us that for
going on two thousand years?

GOWAN'S VOICE (*off-stage*)
Temple.

TEMPLE
Coming.

They exit. The door closes in, clashes, the clash and clang of the key as the Jailor locks it again; the three pairs of footsteps sound and begin to fade in the outer corridor.

(*Curtain*)

EDITORS' NOTE

Faulkner first used the title *Requiem for a Nun* in a letter to his publisher, Harrison Smith, in October 1933, telling him that he had "another bee now, and a good title, I think: REQUIEM FOR A NUN. It will be about a nigger woman. It will be a little on the esoteric side, like I LAY DYING." In December 1933 Faulkner wrote at least three manuscript pages (two different versions of an opening) of a work by that title, though these pages provide inconclusive evidence about whether it was to be a sequel to *Sanctuary* or whether it bears any other relationship to the 1951 novel.

On February 11, 1949, Faulkner began writing *Requiem for a Nun* as a play for his friend Ruth Ford, who had asked him to write a play for her and whose "terrifying determination to be an actress" he had long admired. By this time he had also met an aspiring young writer named Joan Williams, whom he proposed to make a protégé by getting her to collaborate with him. By May 19, 1950, he had reconceived the work as a novel in three acts, each act preceded by a long prose narrative recounting the history of Yoknapatawpha County and Mississippi. He completed the novel by June 1, 1951, and it was in galleys by June 13.

At Faulkner's instructions, Robert Linscott of Random House sent a set of galleys to Ruth Ford. During the summer of

1951, Faulkner, Ford, and director Albert Marre met in New York and in Cambridge, Massachusetts, to adapt the novel to the stage. As Faulkner worked on the stage version, he made extensive revisions to the galleys of the novel, returning them to Random House with numerous attached carbon typescript sheets containing text that was to replace the text as originally submitted. Thus copy-text for the Polk text of *Requiem for a Nun* is a combination of Faulkner's original typescript and these new sheets from the play script, as they revised the galleys. *Requiem for a Nun* was published on September 7, 1951, in a text marred by a large number of typographical errors and several unfortunate editorial alterations. (The stage version, credited to Faulkner and Ruth Ford, was published by Random House in 1959.)

The following notes were prepared by Joseph Blotner and are reprinted with permission from *Novels 1942–1954* (1994) in the edition of Faulkner's collected works published by The Library of America. Numbers refer to page and line of the present volume (the line count includes chapter headings). No note is made for material included in the eleventh edition of *Merriam-Webster's Collegiate Dictionary.* For more detailed notes, references to other studies, and further biographical background, see: Joseph Blotner, *Faulkner, A Biography,* 2 vols. (New York: Random House, 1974); Joseph Blotner, *Faulkner, A Biography, One-Volume Edition* (New York: Random House, 1984); *Selected Letters of William Faulkner* (New York: Random House, 1977), edited by Joseph Blotner; and Calvin S. Brown, *A Glossary of Faulkner's South* (New Haven: Yale University Press, 1976).

5.2.–10 Harpes . . . Murrel] The brothers William Micajah "Big" (1768–99) and Wiley "Little" (1770–1804) Harpe, Samuel Mason (1750?–1803), and John Murrel (or Murrell or Murel; 1804?–?1850).

79.3 (*Beginning Was* τὸ 'ἐν)] Faulkner wrote in a note to his publisher that this was a paraphrase of T. S. Eliot, "Mr. Eliot's Sunday Morning Service": "In the beginning was the Word. / Superfetation of τὸ 'ἐν (τὸ 'ἐν is Greek for "the one").

82.29 Hare] Mississippi outlaw Joseph Thompson Hare.

84.6 p.c.] Post of command.

84.21 Doak's Stand] The Doak's Stand Treaty, signed October 18, 1820, in present-day Madison County, Mississippi, provided for the purchase by the United States of about 5.5 million acres of Choctaw territory in western and central Mississippi.

84.27–29 'Leflore' . . . Rabbit] Greenwood Leflore (1800–65) was one of the Choctaw leaders who signed the treaty of Dancing Rabbit Creek on September 27, 1830. The treaty ceded all remaining Choctaw land east of the Mississippi to the United States in exchange for lands in the western Indian Territory (present Oklahoma). Most of the Choctaw Nation was forced to migrate west between 1831 and 1833, but Leflore remained in Mississippi and became an American citizen.

AS I LAY DYING

As I Lay Dying is Faulkner's harrowing account of the Bundren family's odyssey across the Mississippi country-side to bury Addie, their wife and mother. As they carry Addie in a homemade coffin, pulled along by a team of mules, the Bundrens are haunted by greed and fear—their journey both mocks and confirms our humanity. Their story is told in turn by each of the family members—including Addie herself—as well as those they encounter on their way. This fractured viewpoint epitomizes Faulkner's visceral modernist style, as the varied voices reveal secrets, expose desires, and bring back the dead. A benchmark achievement and one of the most influential novels in American fiction, *As I Lay Dying* not only endures but prevails.

Fiction/Literature

A FABLE

A Fable won both the Pulitzer Prize and the National Book Award in 1955. An allegorical story of World War I, set in the trenches in France and dealing ostensibly with a mutiny in a French regiment, it was originally considered a sharp departure for Faulkner. Recently it has come to be recog-nized as one of his major works and an essential part of the Faulkner oeuvre. Faulkner himself fought in the war, and his descriptions of it "rise to magnificence," according to *The New York Times*, and include, in Malcolm Cowley's words, "some of the most powerful scenes he ever con-ceived."

Fiction/Literature

FLAGS IN THE DUST

The complete text of Faulkner's third novel, published for the first time in 1973, appeared with his reluctant consent in an abridged version in 1929 as *Sartoris*.

Fiction/Literature

THE SOUND AND THE FURY

The Sound and the Fury is the tragedy of the Compson family, featuring some of the most memorable characters in literature: beautiful, rebellious Caddy; the manchild Benjy; haunted, neurotic Quentin; Jason, the brutal cynic; and Dilsey, their black servant. Their lives fragmented and harrowed by history and legacy, the character's voices and actions mesh to create what is arguably Faulkner's masterpiece and one of the greatest novels of the twentieth century.

Fiction/Literature

ALSO AVAILABLE

Absalom, Absalom!
Big Woods
Collected Stories
Go Down, Moses
The Hamlet
Intruder in the Dust
Knight's Gambit
Light in August
The Mansion
Pylon
The Reivers
Sanctuary
Three Famous Short Novels
The Town
The Uncollected Stories of William Faulkner
The Unvanquished
The Wild Palms

VINTAGE INTERNATIONAL
Available wherever books are sold.
www.vintagebooks.com

Printed in the United States
by Baker & Taylor Publisher Services